"I'm sorry I lied to you. I'm sorry I hid things from you."

Jake held up a hand. "It's understandable."

"I realized how important it was to tell you everything. But it was more than that." She peeled her hand from the counter and ran it along the tail of his tattoo snaking out of the arm of his T-shirt onto his left forearm. "I knew if I ever hoped to have some kind of relationship with you, I'd have to tell you all about my past."

His arm tensed and corded beneath her fingertips. "Do you hope to have some kind of relationship with me?"

His voice, all rough around the edges, sent a thrill to her core, and Kyra dug her fingertips into his flesh. "I do, if I haven't scared you off."

Keeping his arm in her grip, he hunched forward across the island and wedged a finger beneath her chin. "Do I look like the kind of man who scares easily?"

THE DECOY

CAROL ERICSON

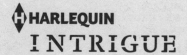
HARLEQUIN
INTRIGUE

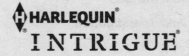

HARLEQUIN®
INTRIGUE®

ISBN-13: 978-1-335-40171-7

The Decoy

Copyright © 2021 by Carol Ericson

Harlequin Enterprises ULC
22 Adelaide St. West, 40th Floor
Toronto, Ontario M5H 4E3, Canada
www.Harlequin.com

Printed in U.S.A.

Carol Ericson is a bestselling, award-winning author of more than forty books. She has an eerie fascination for true-crime stories, a love of film noir and a weakness for reality TV, all of which fuel her imagination to create her own tales of murder, mayhem and mystery. To find out more about Carol and her current projects, please visit her website at www.carolericson.com, "where romance flirts with danger."

Visit the Author Profile page at Harlequin.com.

CAST OF CHARACTERS

Jake McAllister—This LAPD homicide detective has stopped one copycat killer and is on the trail of a second who is mimicking the MO of a murderer from twenty years ago. But the entanglements of the case are nothing compared to the mystery of the woman who's beginning to capture his heart.

Kyra Chase—Her work on the serial killer task force as a victims' rights advocate keeps her close to The Copycat Player case and even closer to its lead detective, and she can't decide which is more important.

Roger Quinn—A retired LAPD homicide detective with one failure on his record—his inability to catch the serial killer known as The Player. But he's tried to make up for it by protecting one of The Player's victims for twenty years.

Billy Crouch—Jake's partner is the levelheaded one of the duo, but he has his own traumas to overcome to be able to do his job.

La Prey—A mysterious stalker who is taunting Kyra with her secrets and seems to know everything about her...and the copycat killers.

The Copycat Player 2.0—A precise serial killer who follows all the rules of the game—except one.

Prologue

Rule number three. Never leave fingerprints or DNA.

He didn't have to worry about that. He was careful and clean. Besides, he'd much rather do the deed in the comfort of their own homes, among their own possessions. It might give them a bit of solace. He was no monster. He was a…facilitator, a conduit, if you will.

Who wanted to traipse all over LA looking for a dump site with a dead body in your car? You could never tell who was watching. Whether a place had cameras or not. Cameras tracked your every move these days. With a little surveillance, you could take care of any electronic witnesses yourself. That was what he did.

And rape? His stomach lurched. Sex was filthy. He would never leave his bodily fluids inside another person.

The woman beneath him gurgled, and he blinked. Time to get back to business.

As he choked the last bit of life out of Andrea with his gloved hands, he watched the light die from her wide eyes. The force of the power that surged through his body made him hard. He closed his eyes to relish the sensation…just for a few seconds of indulgence.

He would never tell anyone about that part—about the sexual arousal. He didn't know why it happened. He didn't ask for it. It wasn't his raison d'être. It made him feel slightly ashamed.

He removed his hands from Andrea's neck and flexed his fingers. It took strength to squeeze the life out of someone. He'd forgotten how much. That other time had been so long ago.

He left Andrea in her bed. She'd been there when he'd pounced, and it had really been more of a creep than a pounce. By the time she realized he was in her house, at the foot of her bed, she had zero time to react or escape.

No, actually, she had reacted—a gaping-mouthed silent scream. The wisps of sleep still clinging to her mind, she hadn't been able to process the sight of a strange man in her bedroom.

The mattress huffed when he pushed off the bed, the same sound Andrea had made when he first took her by the throat. He smoothed a gloved hand over the cap covering his head. He wouldn't be leaving any of his hair behind. No prints. No bodily fluids. He'd taken care to avoid neighborhood cameras. He certainly didn't know Andrea.

That wasn't completely true. He brushed a knuckle across her smooth dark skin. He'd stalked her long enough to know her habits, some of her likes and dislikes, a few of her friends. Long enough to know she'd broken up with a boyfriend and lived alone in this small, neat house. That was as close as he'd gotten— as close as he'd wanted to get.

He wrapped some double-sided tape around his hands and patted the covers around Andrea's body. Who knew what he'd dragged into this room on his person? There could be fibers from his clothing, bits of seed or dirt that could be identified from his area. He'd watched enough forensic crime shows to know anything could be analyzed these days.

He studied the minuscule debris on the tape, peeled it from his hands and shoved it into his pocket. He reached into his other pocket and pulled out a playing card.

Hovering over Andrea, he placed the card between her parted lips. Then he snipped off one of her dark curls and dropped it into a plastic bag. Eyeing his handiwork, he sighed. Now he'd have to create a mess. He hated leaving a mess.

The blade of the box cutter winked at him as it caught the light from the lamp next to Andrea's bed. Holding his breath, he sliced the pinkie finger from her left hand.

The souvenir.

Chapter One

Kyra clutched her throat with one hand. "I don't understand. The Copycat Player is dead. I was there. I saw Jordy Lee Cannon die. You found all the evidence you needed at his mother's house. The jewelry, the box cutter, playing cards."

"But no severed fingers." The phone call announcing another homicide had already propelled Jake to his feet. "We got the right guy, Kyra. This is someone else. Slightly different MO."

"Slightly different?" She scrambled to a crouching position, grabbing the handrail of the bridge that crossed the canal to Quinn's house for support to hoist herself up. "Then maybe it's not a copycat of the…er…Copycat."

Shaking his head, Jake grabbed her hand. He hated that she had to go through all this again. They'd just ended the horrific reign of a murderer who'd been mimicking the MO of a killer from twenty years ago—a killer who'd slaughtered Kyra's mother and never been caught. Now she'd have to face the constant reminders from another sick bastard.

"A playing card in the woman's mouth and a severed little finger. This guy's following the same pattern, except he murdered the victim in her home and left her body there."

Jake's muscles tensed as he looked into Kyra's eyes. Her mother had also been murdered in their home while Kyra slept in the bedroom.

Kyra squared her shoulders. "Then the crime scene should be rich with evidence and you'll catch this guy before he does it again. Because he'll do it again. Jordy managed four victims because he strangled them in his car and dumped their bodies. This guy has already made a big mistake."

Blowing out a breath, he tugged on her hand. "I'm heading over there now. I'll walk you back to Quinn's. Can you get a ride home?"

"Of course, but you should come inside and tell Quinn yourself. I'm sure he'd rather hear this from you."

They walked back across the wooden bridge over the canal where Abbot Kinney had tried to re-create Venice in the middle of a Southern California beach town. The charm of the location and evening was spoiled by the news of another homicide. No wonder he couldn't get to second base with Kyra.

After a few bumps in the road, they'd gotten close working together on the case of the Copycat Player. Her position as victims' advocate on that task force and her tragic ties to the original killer, dubbed The Player, had proved invaluable to the investigation.

Jake hesitated at retired detective Roger Quinn's

red door. Quinn, who had never solved The Player murders twenty years ago, had taken solace in the fact that they'd stopped The Player's copycat. Now they had to go through it again, and Quinn would be asked to relive the case that still haunted him.

Kyra stepped through first, and Quinn glanced up from the flickering blue light of the TV. One look at their expressions, and the lines on Quinn's craggy face seemed to deepen.

"What's wrong with you two?"

Jake held up his phone. "You're not going to believe this, but I just got a call about a homicide with the same MO as The Player—card between the lips and a missing finger."

Quinn's faded blue eyes narrowed. "Oh, I believe it. Seems like The Player has inspired a new generation of killers. It's because I never caught him, never stopped him."

Kyra rushed to Quinn's side and crouched beside his chair. "He killed her in her home. He surely left something behind. They'll get him, just like they got Jordy."

Quinn placed his gnarled hand on Kyra's head and met Jake's eyes. "Hope you haven't dismantled that task force, Detective."

JAKE PULLED UP to the crime scene, where the revolving lights of the emergency vehicles bathed the street in an eerie, familiar glow. He double-parked in front of the modest, well-kept house that would never be the same again and flung open the door of his sedan.

A young man sat on the back of the ambulance, wrapped in a blanket, his head down, legs swinging. Must've discovered the body.

Jake nodded at his partner, Billy Crouch, standing on the porch talking to a uniform. Their division didn't cover this area of the San Fernando Valley, but he and Billy had led the Copycat Player task force and were the go-to guys now every time a playing card and severed finger figured in the crime scene. After Jordy Lee Cannon, he hadn't thought there'd be another.

He took one big step over the yellow tape and strode toward the house. The cheery pot of flowers on top of the air-conditioning unit that jutted from the window made him falter, and he cursed under his breath at the injustice of a life cut short.

His glance took in Billy's casual clothes that still looked runway ready, and he brushed a scuff of dirt from his own jeans. If he'd been home when he'd gotten the call, he would've put on a pair of slacks and an Oxford shirt, at least, but he'd gone casual himself for dinner with Quinn and Kyra. It was supposed to have been a dinner to celebrate the end of the Copycat Player, and now here they were again.

He joined Billy on the porch. "What do we have in there, partner?"

"Young African American woman strangled in her bed. Not much upset. He must've surprised her in her sleep." Billy's mouth flattened into a grimace. "Queen of hearts placed between her lips and left pinkie finger removed."

"Anything else taken? Jordy had been snatching pieces of jewelry from his victims. Anything like that?" Jake pulled a pair of gloves from the black bag over his shoulder and slipped them on.

Billy raised one shoulder. "Too early to tell. Andrea Miles was in bed, pajamas on, makeup off, no jewelry."

Jake crossed the threshold of the house, and his gaze darted around the neat room, framed pictures undisturbed, multicolored pillows propped up against the arms of the couch, a laptop computer charging on a table. "Lived alone?"

"Yeah. Boyfriend moved out recently. He's the one who called in the murder. They were supposed to meet earlier today to sign some paperwork regarding the house, and she missed the meeting."

"This murder didn't happen tonight?" Jake poked his head into the bedroom where Andrea lay on her bed, covers pulled up to her waist. He could see the red face card in her mouth from here. "No sexual assault?"

"Just like the others, and yeah, looks like she's been dead for at least twenty-four hours based on the fixed, dilated pupils, body temperature and lividity." Billy gestured to the patrol officer standing guard over the body. "Can we have the room?"

"Yes, sir." The officer squeezed past them at the door, leaving Billy and Jake alone with the victim.

Jake approached the bed, not touching anything. Billy had already done a preliminary examination of the body, and neither the photographer nor the fingerprint tech had gotten here yet, so he wanted to leave the scene intact for them.

The responding officer had given Billy the low-down, and Jake continued to pick his partner's brain. "No forced entry?"

"Not that they can see at the windows or doors."

"Boyfriend just moved out. Does he still have a key?"

"He does." Billy jerked a thumb over his shoulder. "That's how he got in to discover Andrea had been murdered. He used his key."

"We'll bring him in for questioning." Jake picked up Andrea's left hand—the one now missing a finger. "I mean, he could've staged this to look like a copycat."

"Anything's possible, man." Billy jerked his head up at the sound of footsteps outside the bedroom door. "You need any more time before we invite the hordes in here?"

"I'll take a look around the rest of the house." Jake skimmed his hand across the bedspread, his glove sticking in a couple of areas. "Have you spoken to the boyfriend yet?"

"Not really. He was in shock. That's why I sent him to the ambulance." Billy nudged Jake's arm as he studied his fingertips. "What's wrong? Find something?"

Jake whipped out two tags from a plastic bag and stuck them on the bedspread in two spots. "I felt something here and here. It felt sticky. It could be saliva, semen. Make sure these are preserved and tested."

Billy turned to the door and invited the crime scene investigators hovering there into the room. "Do your thing. Jake, I'll hit up the boyfriend. See if he can form a coherent sentence now."

Jake gave up his spot next to the victim to the techs and backed out of the room. He did an about-face in the hallway and entered another bedroom. This one contained a daybed and a small dresser and looked unused—for the guests Andrea would never have.

He checked the window and the screen on the outside and popped his head into the small closet. Could the killer have hidden here waiting for Andrea to come home? Possible, but how'd he get in to ambush her?

He took a few steps across the living room to another bedroom, which had been converted into an office. This room didn't have a closet, just a desk, filing cabinet and a bookshelf. Crouching down, he read the titles—mostly self-help, yoga and exercise books, and a volume of Langston Hughes poetry. Jake swallowed. A dream deferred, indeed.

A cursory check of the window offered him nothing, and he entered the kitchen. He tried the door next to the pantry, and it opened onto a one-car garage where Andrea's compact waited.

He flicked the switch to his right and light flooded the garage. Andrea's organization skills didn't extend to the garage. Although she'd left enough room to pull her car inside, she'd crammed boxes and bikes and snowboards into the remaining spaces.

He took one step down and felt the hood of the car with his hand. He opened the car door and looked for a garage door opener on the visor. Instead, Andrea's new-model car had buttons that could be programmed to open a garage door.

He punched one, and the garage door started its journey along the tracks. Another stab at the button stopped the door's progress and another brought it back down. The garage door wasn't locked, but it would've made a lot of noise opening. Andrea probably would've heard that.

Jake picked up a crumpled receipt on the console and squinted at the date. Andrea had bought a soda and a bag of chips at a gas station convenience store at 8:46 p.m. yesterday. If she had been dead for about twenty-four hours like Billy thought, this must've been her last trip outside.

Resting his hands on the steering wheel, he murmured, "What happened when you got home, Andrea?"

The door to the kitchen swung open, and a cop stuck his head into the garage. "Is that you, Detective Mac?"

Jake waved his hand out the car door. "Checking out the vehicle."

"Okay, medical examiner is here, and Detective Crouch is done talking to the victim's ex."

"Thanks. I'll be there in a minute."

The cop ducked back inside the house and the

door slammed shut. Jake dropped the receipt into a plastic bag.

He slid from the car and tried the handle of the door back to the kitchen. The handle didn't turn, but he was able to push open the door. He ran his finger over the button on the handle, which was in the locked position.

"What are you doing?" Billy stuck his foot against the door to hold it open.

Jake tapped his fingertip against the wad of gum lodged against the lock tab in the door. "This is how the bastard got in…and he left his DNA."

Chapter Two

Kyra propped up the wall in the back of the conference room as Jake and Billy took turns reviewing the evidence in the Andrea Miles homicide. Most of the equipment from the previous task force hadn't even been removed yet.

Despite her role in the takedown of Jordy Lee Cannon, the Copycat Player, she felt her place was still at the back of the room. Jake hadn't told the rest of the task force that her mother, Jennifer Lake, had been one of The Player's victims twenty years ago, and if she continued to keep a low profile, they'd never find out.

She didn't want to be that girl, and had gone to great pains to put the past behind her and forge a new identity. She didn't need the publicity splashed all over the local news and the internet. That notoriety could only lead to disaster for her.

A wad of gum flashed on the slide. Jake said, "I found this crammed in the lock mechanism of the door that leads from Andrea's house to her garage. If you always keep that door locked, chances are you don't check it. You just let the door close. We believe the killer slipped into Andrea's garage when she pulled out, and then he stuffed the gum in the door she'd left open, which her ex said they did a lot. This gave the killer access to the house at night, where he could lie in wait. When she pulled her car out that last time, he slipped in, gained access to the house and hid out, waiting for her to return and go to sleep."

Kyra crossed her arms against the shiver snaking through her body. That meant the killer must've stalked Andrea long enough to learn some of her habits.

"But—" Jake aimed a red laser at the slide on the screen "—if he chewed this gum to soften it up, we have his DNA and maybe even teeth impressions."

Clive Stewart, the fingerprint tech standing next to Kyra, mumbled, "Idiot. He might as well have left a bunch of prints at the scene."

Kyra moved closer to Clive and whispered, "Which he didn't?"

"Not a one."

Jake and Billy took a few more questions before adjourning the meeting, and several members of the task force moved next door to the conference room, which had been repurposed into the task force war room.

The officers were already calling this killer The Player 3.0. It was either that or Copycat 2.0. What was it about The Player's reign of terror that had so fascinated two killers twenty years later?

As she grabbed the back of her chair in the war room, Jake called, "Kyra, I have Andrea's contacts."

She pushed in the chair and wended her way through the other desks to Jake's. "Is her family here?"

"Her parents are coming out from Atlanta, and two of her friends and her ex have requested some assistance in dealing with her murder." He slid a piece of paper toward her with names and phone numbers printed on it. "We questioned the ex-boyfriend this morning. His alibi is solid. He's also shaken to the core. The breakup was Andrea's idea, and he wasn't over her."

"I'll reach out to them." She shoved the piece of paper in her pocket. "Something else?"

Jake drummed his thumbs on the edge of his keyboard. "Matt Dugan left all of his worldly possessions to you. Did you know that?"

"H-he did?" Kyra pulled her sweater around her body.

"His parole officer called to tell me." Jake shrugged. "You were the closest thing he had to family."

"We were two mixed-up kids in the same foster family at the same time. I'd hardly call that family. I'd hardly call someone who stalks and harasses you family, either." She spun around and called over her shoulder, "Not interested in Matt's worldly possessions, whatever they are."

"That's the thing, Kyra. We don't know what they are."

She stopped her forward movement, but didn't

turn around to face Jake. During the Copycat Player's killing spree, Matt Dugan had left playing cards at her house and car in an attempt to terrorize her over her mother's murder, as her foster brother was one of the few people who knew her real identity. Matt's actions had prompted Jake to go digging into her background…and he probably would've dug further if Matt hadn't died of a drug overdose.

She cleared her throat. "I can assure you, Matt didn't accumulate much of anything during his stints in prison."

"But before he died, he told me someone had paid him to plant those cards for you. Maybe that info is among his effects. Maybe we'll find something, something that will connect that person to Jordy or this current killer."

She turned slowly, still clutching her sweater. "Why would you even think that? Matt was a scammer. He was yanking your chain to up his price for information."

"If there's a chance that there's a clue among Matt's stuff, wouldn't you want to find it if it stops one more murder?" Jake's hazel eyes seemed to probe her soul—he knew where to hit her.

"Of course. I just think you're putting too much faith in a master manipulator. Even this—" she flung out her hand "—leaving his junk to me is a last jab to get under my skin."

He held out an envelope in the space between them. "I got this from his parole officer. It's Matt's handwritten will and a key to his apartment. His roommate still lives there."

"Lucky me." She snatched the envelope from Jake with a hand she hoped he hadn't noticed was trembling. When would she ever get Matt out of her life?

An hour later, she was on her way to Jeremy Bevin's place to discuss his feelings about his murdered ex-girlfriend. As a therapist and victims' rights advocate, she'd worked closely with the LAPD in the past on homicide cases. She had a unique perspective to bring to the table, even though only Jake knew about that.

She'd been eight years old when her mother, Jennifer Lake, had been murdered by The Player twenty years ago. That case had never been solved, despite Detective Roger Quinn's best efforts. Quinn and his wife had wanted to adopt her, but Quinn's alcoholism and probably his age at the time had quashed those plans.

She pulled across the street from Jeremy's apartment and stepped out of the car. She tilted up her nose and sniffed. Despite the sunshine and warmth, fall had crept out from beneath the blanket of oppressive heat that often characterized late summers in LA. Only a true Angeleno could discern the differences between the sunny, blue skies of summer and the sunny, bluer skies of fall. The quality of the air had a slight lilt to it instead of the stillness of waiting. The feel of the sun on her shoulders was more like a light scarf than a beach towel.

Kyra walked across the street and planted herself

in front of the heavy security door of the apartment complex. She trailed her finger down the row of buttons with names neatly typed out beside them and located Jeremy's apartment number. She drilled her thumb against the button, and the lock on the door clicked without a peep from the intercom. He *was* expecting her, but she thought he would have been a little more careful after his ex-girlfriend had just been murdered.

She heaved open the door and stepped onto the cool tile floor. Veering around a group of people carrying bags of groceries, Kyra headed for the elevator. In the style of the sprawling San Fernando Valley, this apartment building didn't have many floors. She rode the elevator to the top and got off on the fourth floor, where the front doors to the units were all tucked into alcoves off the main hallway.

Before she reached Jeremy's door, she heard a click and a rustle, and a young bearded man stepped into the hallway. "You're Ms. Chase?"

"Yes. You can call me Kyra. Can I call you Jeremy?" She took his outstretched hand and gave it a squeeze.

"Yeah, Jeremy's fine." He widened the door for her, and she walked into his bare apartment. He hadn't bothered to put pictures on the wall yet or even unpack boxes, which were stacked in a corner. Hadn't he and Andrea broken up a few months ago?

"Have a seat." He waved in the general direction of two chairs, both facing a flat-screen TV, a small table in front littered with to-go boxes, chip bags and video game controllers.

She'd seen pictures of Andrea's tidy house. Maybe she'd kicked her boyfriend out for reasons of cleanliness, or maybe these were signs of his depression.

She sat in one of the chairs and placed her purse at her feet, gun pouch outward, not that she needed her weapon for a discussion with Jeremy, the jilted boyfriend.

"Do you want something to drink? I got soda in a can or bottled water."

"A soda would be great, thanks." She always wanted her clients to feel she was comfortable so that they could take the cue from her.

Jeremy banged around the kitchen and returned with two cans—a soda for her and a beer for himself. He handed her the drink and cracked the tab on his own.

"You don't mind if I have a beer, do you? I figure that's one of the advantages to having a therapist come see you at home."

"Have you been drinking a lot of beer?" She took a sip of her soda, didn't see a clear space to set it down and so held it in her hand, her fingers tingling from the cold.

"You mean before or after the...murder?"

"Either, both."

"Both. I started drinking more when Andrea and I split up, and I'm not about to stop now that she's dead." To prove his point, he gulped back a quantity of liquid from the can.

"I'm not here to get you to stop drinking, unless that's what you want. As you know, I'm a victims' rights advocate. I'm here on behalf of the LAPD, and I'm here to help you, if you need it or want it."

"I do." He dragged the back of his hand across his mouth. "I don't mean to be an ass. I just feel so… guilty, you know?"

"That's not uncommon, and I can sit here all day and tell you Andrea's death isn't your fault, but you're still going to feel guilty." She wet her lips again with the drink and set the can at her feet. "Tell me about Andrea and your relationship with her."

Her request opened the floodgates, and Jeremy talked about how he and Andrea had met online a few years ago and had bought the house together nine months ago.

"My friends all thought I was crazy to buy the house with her because we fought a lot, but I always had faith in us." He scratched his beard. "It wasn't even because she was Black and I'm white. Our race wasn't the issue, ever. She just always had a lot more going for her than I did, and she expected me to step it up and I never did."

"Had she moved on to someone else?"

"No. That's why I thought we still had a chance. I was hoping our meeting the other day might lead to something. I was going to prove to her that I wasn't stalking her."

Reaching for her soda can, Kyra almost knocked it over. "Excuse me? Someone was stalking Andrea?"

"I don't know. I think she was making it up."

"Making up what, exactly?"

Jeremy dented one side of his beer can with his thumb. "She accused me of trying to scare her into asking me to move back into the house."

"Scare her how?"

"She asked me if I was following her or watching her."

"Did you tell the police about this?"

Jeremy blinked. "No. I kind of forgot about it, honestly. She made her accusations, and I denied them. It was just another way we went around and around. Do you think...?"

"I think it's important enough to tell the police about it. Maybe the killer was stalking Andrea."

Jeremy slammed a fist into his palm. "If I could get my hands on that guy, I'd kill him. Andrea would've taken me back. I know it."

Kyra doubted Andrea had had any intention of taking Jeremy back, but if he wanted to believe that, she wouldn't dissuade him. Instead, she encouraged him to talk about his feelings of rage and revenge.

They wrapped up their conversation after about an hour. Jeremy had even cleaned off the table while she was there and had traded his beer for water. Progress.

As she left, Kyra handed Jeremy one of Jake's cards. "Make sure you call Detective McAllister and tell him what you told me about Andrea's stalker. It could be really important information."

"I will. Thanks, Kyra." He shoved the card in the back pocket of his jeans. "You know, that house is mine now. She hadn't removed me from the title yet, but I don't think I can ever live there."

Kyra said goodbye and returned to her car. As she wasn't sure Jake's business card would ever make it out of Jeremy's pocket and would probably end up in the washing machine, she called Jake herself.

"How'd the session go with Jeremy Bevin?"

"Interesting." Kyra started the engine of her car. "He said something about Andrea having a stalker. Did you get that from him?"

"Not at all. We asked him if she had a new boyfriend or any enemies, and it was a no to everything."

"Andrea thought Jeremy was stalking her to scare her into letting him move back in."

"That's…drastic."

"Yeah, well, he's kind of a dramatic guy. I wouldn't put it past him, and apparently neither did Andrea. Anyway, I gave him your card just in case he lost the one you gave him and told him to give you a call, but he's a lost soul right now."

"I'll keep on top of it." Jake cleared his throat. "Are you going to check out Matt's apartment?"

"You mean to inspect my inheritance?"

"I'm serious, Kyra. I'd like to see what Matt has among his possessions."

Kyra's heart did a somersault. She wouldn't mind seeing what Matt had in his apartment, either, but she'd prefer to do it alone, away from Jake's curious eyes.

"Okay, I'm already out here in the Valley. It won't take me long to get to Matt's place. You can meet me there." She shifted into Drive and pulled away from the curb before she even ended the call. If Matt had anything incriminating about her past in his stuff, she could snag it before Jake even arrived.

She entered Matt's address in her phone and navigated the streets as it chirped out directions. About twenty minutes later she rolled onto a street of matching run-down apartment complexes. Trash cans between buildings overflowed, and broken toys and discarded furniture created an obstacle course along the sidewalks. She slowed down to scope out a parking space as her tires hit pothole after pothole in the asphalt. Leave it to Matt to find a neighborhood where his hardened appearance would barely raise an eyebrow.

She parallel parked her car between an old junker and a monstrous late-model SUV with big, shiny rims and blacked-out windows. As she slid from her car, two men lounging on an abandoned sofa at the curb gave her the once-over. She rested her hand on the gun in her purse and walked past them with a long stride.

Matt's building had no security entrance or lobby, just a dirty courtyard that the residents seemed to use for storage. Kyra stepped over a deflated inner tube and climbed the stairs to Matt's unit.

She held her breath as she knocked on the door. Matt had a roommate, but Kyra was in no mood to exchange small talk with another parolee like Matt.

She knocked once more before inserting the key in the dead bolt. It didn't turn. The roommate hadn't bothered to lock the top lock. She shoved the key into the lock on the door handle, turning it at the same time. She bumped the door with her hip and it opened.

"Hello?" All she needed was for the roomie to come at her from the back, but nothing stirred in the apartment.

She sniffed the air, detecting the skunky smell of weed clinging to the drapes and worn upholstery. She yanked back the curtains at the front window, sending a flurry of dust to swirl in the sunbeams.

She wrinkled her nose. The place wasn't as messy as she'd feared. Maybe because Matt hadn't been here for weeks.

Nothing in this room belonged to Matt, so it didn't belong to her. She tripped over a pair of boots on her way to the bedrooms in the back. She poked her head into the first room she came to and dismissed it. Not Matt's—too neat. She crossed the hall to the room with the door shut and pushed it open. Yeah, definitely Matt's.

The bed remained rumpled from Matt's last night there, and piles of clothes dotted the floor as if he'd undressed and let his clothing drop in small heaps where he stood.

She had no intention of cleaning up Matt's mess. If his roommate wanted to trash the clothes or donate them or whatever, he was welcome to them.

She wandered to the battered nightstand next to the unmade double bed. An empty bottle of whiskey lay on its side, pointing to an ashtray with a few cigarette butts and a wad of dried-out gum.

She opened the drawer, and a few batteries rattled around. There was also a box of condoms and a prescription vial for marijuana.

"Anything good in there?"

She whirled around, nearly slamming her fingers in the drawer, to face Jake, framed by the bedroom door. "You scared me. How'd you get in?"

Holding up a key between his fingers, he said, "Matt's parole officer sent two keys. I kept one for myself."

"Of course you did." She opened the nightstand drawer again to finish her inspection. "What did you need me for?"

"You're the rightful heir. I can't just nose around in here by myself." He stepped into the room and kicked at a pile of clothes. "Find anything of importance?"

"You mean like the phone number or instructions from the guy who paid him to plant those cards for me?" She held up the box of condoms and shook it. "Nope. Just these. Need some?"

She fired the box at him, and his right hand shot out and caught it. He squinted at the writing on the box and tossed them onto the bed. "Not my brand."

Heat touched her cheeks, so she buried her nose farther into the drawer. "Nothing much in here. I think it's more likely that Matt was lying to you about getting paid to torment me with the playing cards. He was just scamming to get more money out of you."

"Maybe." Jake crossed the room to a feminine-looking carved dresser, its mirror hidden by the clothing piled on top of it. With one hand, he swept the clothes onto the floor. "Just like a teenage girl, Matt has some photos stuck in his mirror. And you said he was a cold bastard."

"I didn't even notice those." Kyra joined him and hunched over the dresser. She scanned the mostly old pictures and zeroed in on one of a hodgepodge family at the same time Jake jabbed his finger at it.

"Is that one of Matt's foster families? The foster family you shared?"

Kyra snatched the picture from the mirror. "No. Matt's too young in this picture. He was older when we were in the same family."

"Wonder why he kept that one."

"Maybe it was someplace where he was relatively happy." Kyra left the photo on the dresser. "Do you want to check the closet? I'll look through these dresser drawers, but I think we're on a hopeless mission here."

"Maybe, but it seems strange Matt would go through the trouble of leaving a will with you as his beneficiary if he had nothing to leave you."

Jake turned from the dresser, and Kyra let a small breath escape as she slipped the photo into the pocket of her sweater.

"Probably just his way of messing with me." She opened the top drawer of the dresser and scooped her hands through the jumbled boxers and socks. The corner of an envelope poked one of her fingertips and she shook it free of the underwear covering it.

Keeping the envelope in the drawer, she read the printing on the outside—the name and address of a storage facility in Van Nuys. Squishing the envelope, she traced the edges of a key inside.

She dropped the envelope into the pocket that contained the photo and twisted her head over her shoulder. "Any luck in the closet?"

"Not unless you like leather—a lot of it." Jake slid the closet door closed with a bang. "He did have his motorcycle at the shop with him when he died. That's yours, too. It's a nice Harley."

"Do I look like the Harley type?" She poked a finger into her chest.

Tilting his head, he squinted. "Yeah, I could see you cruising Highway 1 with your blond hair streaming behind you, a pair of these leather chaps encasing your thighs."

"Careful." She shook her finger at him even as a little thrill of pleasure zinged through her veins at the look in his eyes. She dusted her hands together. "Well, I guess that's it. If someone did pay Matt to leave me the cards, we're not going to find any evidence of that here."

"I guess not." Jake scratched his chin as he surveyed the bedroom. "Even for a recent parolee, Matt traveled light."

"Don't forget. Before his stays in the joint, Matt was a foster kid. Traveling light is our modus operandi." She adjusted the strap of her purse on her shoulder. "I'm ready to get out of here."

"Thanks for inviting me along."

"Did I have a choice?" She raised her brows and then swept out of the room. "Maybe you can have Matt's parole officer let his roommate know I'm done here."

"Huh?" Jake emerged from the bedroom, his hand in his jacket pocket. Had he gone back for the condoms?

"I said, Matt's parole officer can tell the roomie he can have Matt's stuff."

"I'll let him know. Now let's get out of here." Jake picked up a prescription medication bottle from the coffee table and shook it. "Matt's roommate probably doesn't mind you coming in here to look around, but he wouldn't be happy to know a cop had been nosing around his place."

As they walked into the apartment's courtyard, Kyra asked, "Did any of Andrea's other friends say anything about a stalker?"

"Not that I know of. We haven't talked to all of them yet."

"And I suppose you don't know if anything's missing from her place."

"Nope." Jake stopped in the middle of the sidewalk between his car and hers.

"What?"

"I always thought it was odd that the Copycat Player took the fingers *and* the jewelry. Most serial killers are satisfied with one trophy."

"And you never found the missing fingers."

Jake shrugged and pulled his car keys from his pocket. "My theory is that he did it to match the MO of The Player, and really didn't care about the fingers."

"I know, but what do you do with a pile of severed fingers?" Kyra hunched her shoulders and clenched her teeth.

"Probably destroyed them or dumped them, but he still had the jewelry. He didn't destroy all the evidence." He jerked his thumb over his shoulder. "My car's back this way. I'll catch up with you later."

She waved as a warm glow kindled in her heart. When Captain Castillo had invited her to join the serial killer task force a few month ago, Jake hadn't been thrilled. He'd been double-crossed by a therapist before and didn't trust them. Now he wanted to catch up with her.

She clicked the remote on her car and slid behind the wheel. She buzzed down her window and waved her hand outside as Jake's car passed hers.

She watched him turn the next corner. Then she pulled the photo from the pocket of her sweater and studied the unhappy faces of the children clustered around a man and a woman—Buck and Lori Harmon.

Buck Harmon had his hands on the shoulders of a young girl, who clung to the hand of an older girl. Lori Harmon held a bawling baby on her hip, her hand on the head of a scruffy boy with a dirt-smudged face, her fingers digging into his scalp, forcing him to face the camera. Matt hovered at the edge of the group, a scowl twisting across his face.

Kyra's nose stung. She pulled a lighter from her pocket, the final item she'd taken from Matt's apartment—her sad inheritance. Holding the picture out the car window, she flicked the lighter and touched the flame to the corner of the picture. The orange fire raced across the photo, eating up the faces and the memories with it.

She let the mini inferno get close enough to her fingers to feel the singe. Then she dropped the picture to the street and drove away.

Chapter Three

Jake waited until he got back to the station before whipping out the remaining photos that had been tucked in the mirror above Matt's dresser. One was missing—because Kyra had taken it.

He shoved his sunglasses to the top of his head and squinted at the first picture, which must be Matt at around the age of six or seven, alone with a scrawny young woman who looked like a hippie. Mom?

Another picture showed the same child, presumably Matt, with a boy and a girl, sitting in a row on a floral sofa, each holding a book among some Christmas wrapping paper.

He shuffled through the rest and put them in order according to Matt's age in each picture, creating a timeline of his foster families. Kyra had the one that should've been at the end, the photo of the foster family she'd shared with Matt.

There had been four or five kids along with parents in that picture, but he hadn't gotten a good look at the tall blonde girl holding the hand of a younger girl because Kyra had snatched it out of his hand too quickly. It made sense, though. Matt and Kyra were the oldest children in that home, teenagers ready to be released to a world that had already discarded them. Matt had gone one way—drug, crime, prison; Kyra had gone another—college, career, success, thanks to the intervention of Quinn and his wife, Charlotte.

Why would she want to hide that picture from him and lie about it? Jake grunted and stuffed the photos in his bag. He thought he and Kyra had gotten past the deception hurdle of their relationship.

He'd had to do his own snooping to figure out Kyra's mother, Jennifer Lake, had been one of The Player's victims twenty years ago and that Kyra had changed her name and identity when she went to college. He'd understood why she'd kept that from him and the rest of the task force, but why all the mystery surrounding her relationship with her foster brother Matt Dugan?

When Dugan had contacted him, it wasn't just about who had paid him to plant the playing cards for Kyra to find. Dugan had also promised him some dirt on Kyra. He hadn't trusted Dugan, but the man had died of a drug overdose before Jake got to him. Kyra had been there at the time he slipped into unconsciousness.

If Matt and Kyra had engaged in some sexual relationship as Matt had hinted, Jake wouldn't care about that. Hell, they'd been two lonely, misplaced teens at the time. Who could blame them for finding solace in each other's arms? Was that why Kyra had snatched the photo? She didn't want any questions about her time in the foster family with Matt?

Jake grabbed his bag and exited his vehicle. Maybe he should just leave it alone. If he and Kyra got…closer, she'd tell him what she wanted to. Still, how could they get closer if she kept hiding things from him?

His marriage had ended because his wife had been cheating on him, and he'd been too busy with work to notice or care. He didn't want to go overboard in the other direction with Kyra.

He stalked into the Northeast Division and dropped into his chair at his computer. He shuffled through a few messages on his desk, pulling out the one from Andrea's ex. He was following through on Kyra's advice. Sometimes Kyra got more out of witnesses and people of interest than hardened detectives. Captain Castillo had recognized her value and assigned her to the serial killer task force for the Copycat Player. Jake had resisted her presence at first, but had come to recognize her value. The insane chemistry between them hadn't hurt, either. Not that they'd acted on it.

And now? She was hiding something from him again.

His fingers flew across the keyboard to access Matt Dugan's data. He didn't have permission to see Dugan's juvenile records, but that didn't mean he couldn't view his file from the Department of Children and Family Services.

He pulled up the DCFS database and could only

get so far. Pushing back from the desk, he crossed his arms. Who did he know in DCFS?

Billy careened into the war room waving a piece of paper. "Hey, partner. We fast-tracked the DNA test on the gum and we have a match."

Jake smacked his desk. "I knew he'd made a mistake. Is it some felon matched in CODIS?"

"Uh, no." Billy parked himself in front of Jake and held out the paper. "It's Jeremy Bevin's, Andrea's ex."

Jake slumped as if someone had just stuck a needle in him and popped him. "Jeremy? He has an alibi, and are you telling me he copied a serial killer's MO to kill his girlfriend?"

"It happens." Billy lifted one stylishly clad shoulder. "And his alibi is his good friend who was helping him set up stuff in his new place. Could be covering for him."

Jake rubbed his eyes. "Probably not, but let's get the footage from his apartment building or street to verify. I need to talk to him, anyway. Let's bring him in."

An hour later, they had Jeremy sweating bullets in an interrogation room while Billy reviewed the security footage from Jeremy's apartment building on the night Andrea was murdered.

The video showed Jeremy and his friend carrying some boxes into the building, leaving and returning with more boxes, a pizza and a six-pack. They didn't leave again that night. The next morning the friend took off and Jeremy left later, presumably for his meeting with Andrea, which never happened.

Billy clicked his mouse to end the tape. Jake, who'd been hunched over Billy's shoulder, straightened up and said, "Alibi is solid."

"Then how the hell did his gum get wedged into that lock?"

"That's what we're going to find out right now." He crooked his finger at Billy and the two of them went downstairs to the interrogation room.

Jeremy jerked his head up when they walked into the room. "Wh-what's going on? Why am I in here?"

Jake yanked out a chair while Billy took up a position in the corner, folding his arms. "I thought you had something to tell me."

"Well, I do, but—" Jeremy's gaze jumped to Billy in the corner, whose smile seemed downright sinister "—why did you stick me in here?"

"We had to check out your alibi, Jeremy." Jake splayed his hands on the metal desk, his thumbs meeting.

"I thought you already called George, and he verified it."

"We did, but someone used chewing gum to muck up a lock so the door from the house to the garage wouldn't lock. We checked the gum for DNA, and it matched the sample we took from you when we first questioned you."

Jake studied Jeremy's face, which blanched first and then heated to a bright red. "Mine? My gum? I wouldn't need to do that. I still have my key."

"Could've done it to throw us off." Jake held up his hands. "But we know you didn't because we looked at the surveillance video from your apartment building. Your alibi checks out."

"Whew." Jeremy wiped his brow and then sat up, shoulders straight. "I mean, of course it did. I told you, I'd never hurt Andrea. I loved her. Still love her."

"The question is, when were you last chewing gum at Andrea's?"

"I *am* a gum chewer." He reached into his pocket and flipped a pack of sugarless gum onto the table. "I'm a former smoker. Gave it up for Andrea."

Billy made an impatient move in the corner. "Okay, we know how much you loved her. Now answer the question. When were you last chewing gum at that house, and do you throw it in the trash or spit it on the ground? And, no, we're not going to arrest you if you admit you spit it on the ground."

"Sometimes I spit it in the gutter. I figure people are less likely to step on it there." Jeremy's fingers nervously fiddled with the pack of gum. "Before I went to Andrea's and found her…body, I was there a few days before that to pick up some boxes from the garage."

Jake gave a sidelong glance to Billy. Was he thinking the same thing? Was the killer watching Jeremy at that point and specifically used Jeremy's gum to implicate him?

They had to collect more video from the area for different times.

Jake nailed down the day and time of that visit, as close as Jeremy remembered, and he sat back in his chair. "Ms. Chase indicated that you told her about a stalker Andrea had?"

Jeremy wiped a hand across his brow as the questioning turned away from him and his visits to Andrea's house. "Yeah, Andrea accused me of following her, but it wasn't me. She didn't get into it that much. Told me to stop following her and coming by the house uninvited. When I denied it, she dropped it. I don't know if she believed me or not."

They probed him for more info, but he clearly didn't know anything else.

Jake scooted back his chair. "You're free to go, Jeremy. If you remember anything else, give me a call, especially if you recall seeing anyone hanging around Andrea's house or neighborhood."

Jeremy stood up so hastily he had to grab the chair before it fell over. "That guy, the one who killed Andrea... He saw me spit out that gum and picked it up to fix the lock and frame me, didn't he?"

"We can't know for sure." Billy pushed off the wall he'd been propping up the entire interview. "But we think this guy was watching Andrea long before he killed her."

KYRA GLANCED UP as Jake, Billy and Jeremy filed out of an interrogation room. They all wore grim expressions, and Jeremy looked a little pale around the lips.

Clutching files to her chest, she raised her eyebrows at Jake as he met her eyes. He gave a quick shake of his head.

She followed the two detectives up the stairs while

Jeremy peeled off and headed for the exit. She quick-ened her stride to catch up to Jake as he entered the task force conference room, which they'd reassem-bled in record time after Andrea's murder.

"Could Jeremy tell you anything more about the stalker?" She tagged along behind Jake as he went to his desk. He slammed down the lid of his laptop, but not before she saw the familiar logo of the LA County Department of Children and Family Ser-vices.

She tapped the lid of the computer with an un-steady finger. "Andrea didn't have a child, did she?"

"No, that's another case." Jake dropped into his chair and swiveled it around to face her. "Take Billy's chair. He's on his way out."

She sat across from Jake, their knees almost touch-ing. "What did you find out from Jeremy?"

Bending his head toward hers, he said, "I don't know if you heard yet, but the DNA on that gum was Jeremy's."

She sucked in a quick breath. "No."

"Doesn't mean much. We verified his alibi, and when we questioned him, he said he chewed gum and had probably spit some out around Andrea's house a few days before her murder."

"So, the killer picked up Jeremy's gum to literally gum up the lock." She raised a hand to her throat. "Do you think the killer knew it was Jeremy's gum?"

"Too much of a coincidence if he didn't. He could've used putty or anything else. He used gum with Jeremy's DNA."

"That means Andrea's fears of a stalker were probably right on. This guy's been watching her—and Jeremy. Maybe Andrea brushed it off, thinking it was Jeremy and she didn't have to worry."

Jake's lips twisted. "She was wrong."

"Did her friends or family say anything about her concerns?"

"We're not done interviewing her friends." He grabbed a cup of coffee and drained it. "Have you been in touch with the family yet? Are they coming out from Atlanta?"

"I have their contact info, but I haven't spoken to them. I sent them an email detailing my services, so I'm going to leave the ball in their court for now." She rose from Billy's chair, cognizant of a few looks being thrown their way.

It wasn't like she and Jake were dating or anything. That dinner at Quinn's house after the Copycat Player case ended didn't count. Hell, they hadn't even shared their first kiss…yet.

Jake formed his fingers into a gun and pointed it at her. "Let me know what you want to do with Matt's Harley."

"You seem extremely interested in that bike. You want it?"

"That seems…wrong, but I'll think about it."

She lifted and dropped her shoulders, and spun around to march back to her own desk in the corner. Maybe the Miles family had responded to her email. Or maybe they were too devastated to function.

She pulled up her chair to the desk and clicked on

the email icon at the bottom of her screen. Nothing from the Miles family. She scanned through a couple of messages and clicked on one with an attachment from an unknown sender.

She squinted at the attachment, which appeared as a thumbnail, and her pulse ratcheted up several notches. It was a photo with a familiar configuration.

Her hand shook as she moved the mouse over the attachment. Holding her breath, she clicked on it. The photo she'd just burned in the street now filled her computer screen—with one difference.

Someone had placed a large black *X* over the face of Buck Harmon.

Chapter Four

With her heart thundering in her chest and echoing in her ears, Kyra closed the attachment. She scanned the body of the email, which was blank, and the email address. The message had come from one of the free email providers with a display name of LAPREY.

What did that mean? LA prey? Was she supposed to be prey? She felt like it. Twisting her head over her shoulder, she swallowed the lump in her throat that threatened to turn into a howl.

She caught Jake's eye and gave him a weak smile. She couldn't blame this prank on Matt. Had her foster brother been telling Jake the truth when he said that someone had paid him to taunt her with those cards? If so, was someone else being paid to send her threatening emails?

Was it a threat? Blackmail? If it was blackmail, she didn't know what anyone would want from her. She didn't have any money. No influence. No power.

She dropped her chin to her chest. In fact, she hadn't felt this powerless in a long time.

A touch on her shoulder had her jumping out of her seat.

"Whoa." Jake stepped back. "Sorry I startled you. Are you all right?"

And just like he'd done before with his laptop, she snapped her lid shut. "I'm fine. You scared me."

His brows furrowed over his nose. "I meant a few minutes ago when you looked at me across the room. I thought you were sending me an SOS signal."

"Really?" She snorted. "I think you're just over here checking on that Harley. What do you think I could get for it?"

"Probably twenty grand." He balanced one hip on the corner of her desk. "That's not why I crossed the room."

She flipped her hair over her shoulder. Had she really been sending out an SOS? "I'm okay, just stressed like everyone else in this room."

"Do you want to meet me at Quinn's tonight? I'd like to update him on this murder, get his thoughts. I can pick up dinner or even cook for everyone."

Did he feel safe with her only in the presence of Quinn? What did he think would happen if they were alone together? She could think of several things she'd like to do with him in private.

She coughed. "Cook? Quinn wouldn't expect that, and neither would I. You can order in—just no Chinese. Too much sodium for him."

"He's lucky to have you."

"Ah." She raised one finger. "I'm the lucky one."

"Is that a yes, then? You, me, Quinn, dinner at

his place at seven thirty. You can set that up?" With his last syllable, he kept his lips pressed together as if holding his breath.

That sounded…romantic. She pasted on a bright smile. "I'll give him a call. I haven't spoken to him since we left his place the other night when you got the news about Andrea."

"Great." He rapped his knuckles on her desk. "I'll see you at seven thirty…at Quinn's."

He had added that last part hastily when his partner walked by, bumping Jake's shoulder.

The two of them, heads together, walked to their desks, and Kyra returned to her computer and the problem in front of her.

She eased up the lid on her laptop and opened the message. She clicked on the email address and sucked her bottom lip between her teeth as she studied the properties, which told her nothing. She needed to pick the brain of a computer geek to find out who'd sent this message.

Her gaze darted around the room, bustling with phone calls, mini conferences and conversations around the whiteboards, and settled on Brandon Nguyen, the LAPD's tech guy. Just like she'd done with Clive Stewart, the fingerprint tech, she might be able to get Brandon to do a little favor for her—off the radar.

As she watched Brandon, he dropped to the floor, to check some cables, no doubt. She kept her eye on him until he popped up again, brushing the knees of his jeans. He waved a cable in the air and left the war room.

Hastily Kyra jumped from her chair and followed him into the hallway, where she saw Brandon veer into the lunchroom. Perfect.

She walked in on him studying the snack machine. Holding up a dollar bill, she said, "It's on me if I can ask you a question about something."

"Not necessary." He threaded his own money into the machine and punched a couple of buttons. "You can ask me anything, free of charge. That's what I'm here for."

"It's not something related to the case, though, and it is something I'd prefer to keep hush-hush." She sidled up next to him in front of the snack machine and fed her bill into the slot.

Brandon glanced over his shoulder as if she'd just asked him to spill government secrets. He might be a harder nut to crack than Clive had been with the fingerprints. "Um, I guess I can help out, as long as it's not something illegal, you know, like accessing classified information."

She giggled as she selected a granola bar from the rows of junk food. "Of course not. I got an email from an unknown email address, and I'd like to find out where it came from. It's regarding a patient of mine."

That was not a lie. She was her own patient—had been under her own care for years.

His face cleared, and he skimmed a hand through

his black hair. "I can help with that. I have some other work to do right now, though."

"Oh, I didn't mean right this minute. Hit me up when you're free. I should be in the war room for most of the afternoon." She retrieved her granola bar from the tray and pointed it at him. "Thanks a bunch."

Two things being in foster care had taught her was how to be adaptable and agreeable. She could be anyone's best friend in the blink of an eye.

She took her seat in the conference room once again, keeping one eye on the clock and one eye on Jake. She didn't want him to see Brandon working with her because he'd ask questions, and she didn't want to lie to him any more than she had to.

She did place a call to Quinn, who was only too happy to have company tonight, especially if it involved a lowdown on the new case. Quinn might be retired, but he still took a keen interest in all things LAPD Homicide.

Finally Jake and Billy grabbed their jackets in unison and made for the door. Jake made a detour at her desk. "Everything set with Quinn?"

"It is." She wagged her finger between him and Billy, who was waiting at the door. "Where are you two off to?"

"If Andrea had a stalker, and it looks like she did, we're going to check for more cameras in that area. Maybe one of the neighbors caught the guy lurking around earlier."

"I hope so. Good luck." She wiggled her fingers in the air. "'Bye, Billy."

Billy gave her a big grin. She held a special place in his affections after facilitating an introduction between him and her friend Megan Wright, a TV reporter for KTOP. As far as she knew, they were still dating but keeping it light. She wished she could say the same for her and Jake. Did having dinner at Quinn's house talking serial killers count as a date?

About thirty minutes after Jake and Billy left, Brandon approached her, eyebrows raised. "I have some time right now before I leave."

"Great." She scooted her chair over while wheeling another in front of her computer. "Have a seat."

As Brandon adjusted the height of the chair, Kyra reached across him and brought up the email. Although he could probably tell the attachment was a picture from the thumbnail, he wouldn't be able to make out the faces. Wouldn't mean anything to him, anyway.

"This is the message, and that's the email—laprey at newmail dot com."

Brandon brushed some straight bangs from his eyes. "That name mean anything to you?"

"Nope." She wouldn't give him her theory about being prey in LA. "Can you track the IP address, or whatever?"

Brandon clicked around the screen with a speed she couldn't hope to follow. "There are a few things I can do. Can I forward this to myself?"

"Without the attachment. It's confidential."

"Sure, sure." He clicked the button to forward the message, and with his mouse he circled the prompt that asked if he wanted to include the attachment. He clicked No. "I need to perform a few functions on this message with programs you don't have on your laptop."

"Understood. Thank you, so much. Coffee, lunch, those disgusting flaming hot things you like from the vending machine…" She jerked her thumb at her chest. "I'm your girl."

Brandon nodded as he walked the chair back to its rightful place. "I'll remember that."

When he left, Kyra packed up her work and tossed the granola bar in her desk drawer. She'd get to the bottom of this one way or another.

Matt had died of a drug overdose before he could tell Jake who'd paid him to leave the playing cards for her—before he could tell Jake any of her secrets. Who else besides Matt and Quinn knew those secrets? Matt could've told someone before he died, someone ready and willing to pick up where Matt left off. But why? She understood Matt's motivation. He'd been obsessed with her and didn't know whether to love her or hate her half the time. Why would some random person be interested in tormenting her about her past, and why would these events coincide with copycats taking up where The Player had left off?

Maybe Matt told someone she had money. She shrugged her ponytail from her shoulder. "Yeah, good luck with that."

"With what?"

She glanced up, meeting Captain Castillo's dark, intelligent eyes. She had to be careful around all these detectives.

"Ugh, you caught me talking to myself."

"I hope that doesn't mean you need therapy." Castillo winked.

"Any therapist will tell you we all need therapy."

"Just thought I'd drop by to see how you're doing. Everything going okay with… Jake?" Castillo looked down as he ran a hand over his tie.

Her pulse jumped and she schooled her face. "Why do you ask? Has he been complaining about me?"

"Not at all. From the looks of things, he appreciates your work with the task force. I mean, you practically caught the Copycat Player single-handedly, didn't you?"

Her cheeks burned. "You mean by almost becoming one of his victims until Jake rescued me? I hope you don't… I h-hope nobody thinks I believe I'm responsible for his apprehension. I hope Jake doesn't think that."

"Never mentioned it to me. I was joking about the rest. Nobody thinks that." Castillo clenched his hands in front of him, and she waited expectantly.

What did he really want?

"Anyway, everything's going great. The team is as welcoming as ever…" She let her voice trail off and pushed back from her desk.

"Do you still see Quinn?"

"I was good friends with his wife. I see him often." She cocked her head and waited. Did he have a message for Quinn?

"Good to hear someone's keeping track of him." Castillo dabbed at a dried spot of coffee on his yellow shirtfront. "Sorry to keep you."

"No problem. Thanks for checking in. I appreciate your recommendation to the first task force."

He leveled a finger at her. "What you do adds value to an investigation. I firmly believe that."

"Thanks, Captain."

She waited until he had left the room, after chatting with a couple of the officers, and then released a long breath. That was weird. Had he heard something bad about her? Did he want to check on her ties with Quinn before lowering the hammer on her?

If he did, she'd find out later. Right now she had one patient to see before meeting Jake at Quinn's, and she didn't want to leave those two alone together for too long.

JAKE HELD UP the bags of food on his way to Quinn's kitchen. "Hope you like Mediterranean—chicken skewers, rice, hummus. Kyra told me to hold off on the Chinese because of the sodium."

Quinn shook his head. "Damn, that girl treats me like an invalid. You want a beer before she gets here and gives me the evil eye?"

Jake swung the bags onto the counter. "As long as she's not going to transfer that evil eye to me for encouraging you."

Quinn held on to the edge of the counter. "Hell, we're two grown men, LAPD homicide detectives, stared down the baddest of the bad. We're gonna let some slip of a blonde control us?"

Jake stopped fussing with the bags and cocked one eyebrow. "Really?"

"You're right. Let's have those drinks before she gets here."

Chuckling, Jake plunged into the fridge and emerged with two cold ones. He twisted off both lids and slid a bottle across to Quinn.

Quinn raised his beer. "To that slip of a blonde."

"I'll drink to that." Jake tapped the neck of his bottle with Quinn's and took a long gulp. Not that he was trying to get Quinn drunk or anything before Kyra got here, but it might be interesting to talk to the old detective without her hovering, and a couple of beers could facilitate that conversation.

As the two detectives faced each other across the counter, Jake told Quinn about Andrea's murder.

"The playing card was between the lips, and the pinkie finger was missing. We're not sure if any other trophy was taken. Andrea was in bed sleeping when he made his move, so presumably no jewelry. Her ex-boyfriend didn't indicate she slept with jewelry on."

"He's striking out on his own." Quinn scraped the blue foil label from the damp bottle with his fingernail.

"What do you mean?" Jake always felt like a novice sitting at the feet of a master when talking to Detective Roger Quinn—yet Quinn had not solved the case of The Player. Jake didn't know how that would feel. He had a perfect record with every homicide he'd worked.

Must be hell.

"The Copycat Player followed The Player's MO up to a point. The Player never took jewelry and the Copycat decided he would. Now, this guy is following The Player, and not the Copycat. He wants to be his own man in some regards."

"Then why follow him at all?"

Quinn rolled a shoulder. "Notoriety? I don't know. You're the hotshot detective now. You figure it out."

"I plan to. Computer Forensics is still going through Cannon's stuff to see where he got his ideas. They're searching to find out if he was reading up on The Player's case, but even if he was, he wouldn't have learned about the missing fingers from any news stories. You guys kept a tight lid on that."

"And yet here we have another killer who knows about it. I guess the lid wasn't that tight." Quinn spread his hands on the counter, his fingers like misshapen twigs against the tile. "Or word got out. It does."

"This guy was stalking Andrea, murdered her in her home, just like a few of The Player's killings." Jake took a swig of beer. "Interesting how the first copycat, Cannon, chose to kill the victims in his car and dump their bodies, like The Player's first few victims, and now this guy is killing in their homes, like The Player's next few victims. These guys really know their serial killer lore, don't they?"

"Sick bastards." Quinn shoved aside the glittering pile of foil he'd peeled from the bottle. "I'd better get rid of this evidence before Kyra gets here."

Jake drummed his fingers on the counter. "Kyra's mother was murdered in her house, wasn't she?"

Quinn's hands froze in midsweep. "She was. Rented a small house in Hollywood."

"And Kyra was home."

"She was home—sound asleep. Never woke up. The killer probably didn't even know she was there."

Jake doubted that. If The Player had stalked Jennifer Lake, just like Andrea had been stalked, he would've known about a child. He wasn't that careless. Still, he'd be damned if he'd correct the old detective. That would be close to sacrilege. He clamped his lips shut.

Quinn pointed to a cupboard to the right of Jake's head. "Why don't we surprise Kyra tonight and set the table."

"I can do that." Jake pivoted to his right and opened the cupboard door. He grabbed a stack of three plates. "What was Kyra like when you first met her?"

"Traumatized. She'd lost her mother, her world. Jennifer Lake maybe didn't make all the right choices as a mother, but she loved her daughter. Kyra cried for her often." Quinn's faded blue eyes shimmered with the memory.

"And after?" Jake skirted around Quinn's sagging body and put a plate on each of the three place mats on the table. "What was she like when the shock… wore off?"

"I don't know that it ever did." Quinn took his turn in the kitchen and gathered silverware and napkins. "The murder affected her, of course. As a child, she was tough and unafraid, sassy, assertive. Then she learned to submerge all that beneath a sheet of ice—her layer of protection."

"Yeah, I'm familiar with that ice."

Quinn poked him in the arm with a fork. "Keep trying, boy—there's a vibrant, caring woman beneath that veneer."

"You love her like a daughter, don't you?" Jake rubbed his arm where the tines had pricked him.

"I do, even though she was never officially ours. I blame myself for that. If it hadn't been for my abuse of the booze at that time, we might've gotten her."

"Maybe that played a role, but your age and the fact that you were the detective on her mother's murder case probably also had something to do with it. Shouldn't blame yourself."

"But that's what we fathers do, isn't it?"

Jake's eyebrows shot up. "You know I'm a father?"

Quinn nudged his arm with his pointy elbow. "You didn't think I'd let my girl fall for someone without doing my own investigating, do you?"

Chapter Five

Kyra banged on Quinn's door louder than she intended after seeing Jake's sedan parked illegally on the street and discovering the front door was locked. So, he had beaten her there and then locked her out.

"Hello, it's me."

As she scrabbled in the bottom of her purse for the key to Quinn's house, the door flew open and Jake filled the frame like he owned the place.

"It's about time." He swept his arm to the side to gesture her through the door as if she hadn't been here a hundred times before.

Bustling into the house, she said, "About time? I'm right on time. You're early."

She tripped to a stop as she took in the table, set for three, a vase of flowers pulled from Quinn's front yard in the center.

It looked a little bit more like a date in here than to-go containers balanced on their laps in the living room as they discussed serial killers. She approved. "Nice."

"We were just talking about...Andrea." Quinn pulled out a chair at the table and waved her into it.

Kyra shifted a quick glance from Quinn to Jake, suppressing a comment with a pursing of his lips.

Jake nodded, instead. "Getting him up to speed."

"Any insight, Quinn?" Kyra took the proffered chair, nose in the air sniffing the spicy aroma of the food steaming on her plate.

"Just that he's still mimicking The Player with the stalking of a victim and killing her in her home."

"Just like my mom." Kyra sniffed and it wasn't the food.

Quinn joined her at the table and squeezed her hand. "Just like Jennifer."

Jake put a beer in front of each of them, along with a basket of pita bread. "Quinn thinks this guy probably took a trophy from Andrea, even though we haven't found what it could be yet."

"You mean in addition to the severed finger?" Kyra ran a thumb down her bottle of beer without taking a sip. "Just because the Copycat Player did? You think it's jewelry again?"

"The way Quinn explained it to me is that the killer would want a trophy for himself, just like the Copycat Player took the jewelry. That was for him."

"And the finger was for...?" She jabbed at a piece of lettuce on her plate, skewering a small crumble of feta cheese with it.

"For the...game." Quinn took a small sip of his beer, and Kyra knew it wasn't his first. His first drink always resembled that of a man slaking his thirst after a long drought. She and his doctor always cautioned him about the wisdom of an alcoholic testing himself every day with just one or two beers.

"You think the killers are playing some kind of game? Wait." She suspended her fork halfway to her mouth, and the cheese rolled off and fell to her plate. "Do you think Jordy Cannon and Andrea's killer are or were in touch somehow?"

Jake dropped his fork with a clatter. "Is that what you think, Quinn? Is that what you meant by taking his own trophy?"

"Think about it." As if he were taking tea with the queen, he held up his own pinkie finger from the hand wrapped around his bottle. "These killers leave the playing card and then cut off the fingers because they're following the game plan of The Player, twenty years ago. But what do *they* get out of it? The Player had his own sick reasons for severing the fingers and taking them as trophies—reasons we never sorted out. Jordy and this guy don't have those same compulsions, but they're following the same playbook. That's not a coincidence. They know each other, or are part of some sick club."

"They do have different compulsions." Jake scooped up a glob of chicken and rice with a triangle of pita bread and shoved it in his mouth, his appetite clearly not inhibited by the talk of killers and their trophies.

Why would it be? He ate this stuff for breakfast and she, unfortunately, snacked on it.

Quinn shrugged. "Different compulsions, different trophies, different victims."

"But the same MO, copied from The Player. Why would they know each other? The Player's MO is available to anyone with a computer and internet access." She grabbed her bottle. Maybe she needed the booze after all.

"Except the detail about the severed finger is not on the internet. It was kept out of the news." Jake's hazel eyes glowed green around the edges of his irises, as if the ideas behind those eyes were sparking like electrical circuits.

"Quinn, and even you, said those details had a way of leaking out."

"To two different people who both happen to be killers?" Jake planted his elbows on either side of his plate, his appetite on hold.

"If you're buying into Quinn's theory that these killers know each other, you'd better start looking more closely into Jordy's friends."

"That's just it." Taking a swig of beer, Jake settled back in his chair. "Jordy Lee Cannon had no friends."

Quinn steepled his fingers, their crookedness making for a dilapidated church spire. "What's a friend these days? People fall in love online without ever meeting each other in person. I've seen those shows."

Kyra let her mouth drop open in mock outrage. "You watch reality TV dating shows?"

Quinn chuckled. "Only while channel surfing."

"Quinn's right. I'm going to order the full forensics report on Jordy's computer." Jake raised his bottle to Quinn. "I knew it was a good idea coming here."

They finished their dinner in a more normal fashion—discussing the Dodgers' chances of making it to the World Series next month and wondering if they'd have another blast of heat and high winds before SoCal settled down to cooler fall temps.

Kyra offered to clean the kitchen, knowing she could get it done faster than Jake and with the key to Matt's storage container burning a hole in her purse. She had to get out there before Matt's parole officer or roommate or even Jake. She didn't put it past him to get more info from the parole officer and not share it with her. Just like she had no intention of sharing this with Jake.

"Do you two want to take a walk on the canals? I can run the dishwasher, Kyra, and I promise I won't crack open another beer."

She emerged from the kitchen and patted Quinn on the arm, her heart softening. She got it. He wanted to play matchmaker just like on those reality TV shows he claimed not to watch.

Another time and she'd jump at the chance to cozy up to Jake while walking the bridges of Venice, but tonight she had a mission.

"I'm down for that. I could use some fresh air." Jake rose from his chair and stretched, his sage-green T-shirt clinging to the shifting muscles of his chest, giving her a tantalizing look at what she was turning down.

"You know, I'd like that, but I have some work

waiting for me at home." She twisted her lips, not even feigning the regret. "Patient files."

Jake shoved his hands in the pockets of his jeans, his eyes narrowing to slits, giving her the same look as her stray cat when she shooed it outside.

"I've got farther to travel than you, so I'll hit the road." He grasped Quinn's hand. "Thanks for the insight, sir."

"Thanks for the food…and the beer." Quinn winked.

Kyra waved a dish towel at them. "You guys don't fool me one bit. I know you had a beer before I got here."

"Busted." Jake grabbed his weapon and slung the holster over his shoulder, looking like a gunslinger from the Old West—all steely-eyed determination and set jaw.

He didn't look happy that she'd shut him down. He'd be even less happy if he knew why.

Raising his hand, Jake said, "Good night, you two."

The door shut, and an unaccustomed silence hung between her and Quinn for several seconds.

Quinn broke it with a cough. "He's a good guy, Kyra, and he already knows about your mother. No need to shy away like you usually do."

"It's not that. I really do have work to do. Besides, the last stroll we had around the canals ended with a phone call about a dead body."

"Superstitious?"

"Perhaps, and I know he's a good guy. Maybe

that's why it's best we don't go down this road. You
know he has an ex-wife."

"And a daughter, so why are you selling yourself short? You deserve someone in your life, Kyra.
Someone good."

"Do I?" She stooped to kiss him on the cheek. "I
have to run. Don't fall asleep in your chair."

Back in her car, she picked up her phone, punched
in the address of Matt's storage facility and took off.
Forty minutes later, she pulled up to the closed gate.
The card in the envelope must be for after-hours access, and Kyra let out a breath as she shoved the card
in the slot and the gate rolled open.

Matt had even written the number of the storage
unit on the envelope. He must've been expecting a
return visit to the slammer to rent this space.

Following the signs posted at each corner, she
navigated to Matt's unit, nestled along a row of the
smaller containers. These had silver rolltop doors
with a keyhole on the right-hand panel on the outside.

She parked perpendicular to the door of the unit
and scrambled from the car, her heart tapping out
a staccato beat. She'd left her headlights on to aug-
ment the yellow light that spilled from a bulb every
four containers.

With unsteady hands, she inserted the key in the
lock and clicked it to the right. The door rattled as if
to say, *Come on in. I've been waiting for you.*

She bent over, grasped the handle and yanked up,
a muscle in her back jumping in protest. The door
squealed as she raised it, and she held her breath, ex-

pecting some sort of sick joke from Matt to pop out at her. The only joke was that the unit didn't have lighting, but she did have her cell phone.

Standing at the entrance, panting slightly, she scanned the contents of the storage unit with the beam of light from her phone, her gaze tripping over boxes, a few old suitcases and motorcycle parts. If he had anything in here about payment from someone to leave cards for her or anything like that, she'd turn it over to Jake, but she doubted Matt would've stored something so recent. These looked like the past, not the present.

She took a tentative step into the space and sneezed. Did he have more photos in those boxes? Who knew Matt Dugan had been so sentimental about his messed-up foster families?

She practically stumbled over the first row of boxes and dropped into a crouch. She lifted the lid from one of the boxes and shone her light inside, picking out a mass of papers.

She shuffled through the drawings and sketches, her heart lodged in her throat. She'd forgotten about Matt's artistic talent, which had been submerged beneath his fear and resentment and hate. She'd had those same feelings being shuffled among families who'd regarded her with a mixture of pity, horror and greed.

She capped the box and plunged into the next one. This one contained a sort of jumbled filing system with Matt's court dates and releases, and communications with his court-appointed attorneys.

She picked her way through some bike parts, probably stolen, and settled in front of another couple of boxes. She tipped the lid off the first one, which contained more items Matt had probably stolen from the garage. Kyra choked on the oily fumes that rose from the rags wrapped around gadgets and parts that must have been of some use on a motorcycle at one point. She felt behind a greasy carburetor where the box lid had fallen, and then froze as she read the black-scrawled label on the box next to this one. *Mimi Lake.* Her nickname when she was a child, her real last name, the last name tied to a murdered woman.

With dread thrumming through her veins, she tipped up the lid of the box bearing her name. Her hands clawed through the newspaper clippings and candid photos of her long after she'd become Kyra Chase. Her stomach heaved and she pressed a fist against her mouth. Why?

A metal scraping sound at the door of the storage unit caused her to spin on her heels and topple to the side. She frantically reached for the gun tucked in the purse that was slung around her body.

"Did you find what you were looking for?"

Jake's voice reverberated in the metal container.

Desperation and rage had her reaching past her gun for another item in her purse. Without thinking, she flicked the lighter and dropped it on top of the open box. Fueled by the old paper, the flames shot up past the rim of the box, the heat instant on her cheeks.

"Look out!" Jake shouted from the entrance and took a step into the unit.

As Kyra scrambled to her feet, the fire jumped into the second box—the one full of oily rags.

The explosion threw her off her feet.

Chapter Six

The boom reverberated in Jake's ears, bouncing off the metal walls of the storage unit. He stumbled back from the searing heat that blasted his face. The flames raced to the ceiling of the storage unit, and black smoke billowed toward him in a noxious cloud.

The explosion had thrown Kyra away from the fire. She was crabbing backward to escape it, but the flames chased her, licking at her shoes.

Jake lunged forward and grabbed Kyra under the arms. He yanked her once, her legs flying off the ground, and then he dragged her out of the container to the cool air and her car.

Her car. If the fire reached her car, that explosion in the storage unit would seem like a firecracker in comparison.

Smoke abrading his throat, he choked out, "The keys."

In an equally strangled voice, she answered, "In the ignition."

He gave her a hard shove. "Get away and call 911."

He watched her stumble away before jumping into

the car and cranking on the engine. He threw it into gear and stomped on the accelerator. The car leaped backward, and he propelled it away from the blazing storage unit.

As he exited the vehicle, he heard sirens. He swiveled his head, the smoke stinging his eyes and invading his nostrils, but he couldn't see Kyra. His head jerked back to the unit, now belching orange flames and black smoke in some kind of Halloween extravaganza.

She hadn't foolishly gone back inside to save something, had she?

He had taken one step in the direction of the inferno when someone grabbed his arm.

"Where are you going?" Kyra stared at him through soot-ringed eyes that a Goth teen princess would envy.

Before he had a chance to sheepishly admit that he was going back for her, fire engines blared their warning, and he and Kyra moved out of the way.

She held up a card. "I was going to let them through the gate, but the owner had already gotten a fire warning and remotely released the gates for the fire trucks."

Jake peered back at the fire being fueled by Matt Dugan's only earthly possessions. "The corrugated metal should keep the fire from spreading to other units."

"I hope so." She shoved back strands of hair from her loosened ponytail, smearing more soot across her face.

Turning his back on the busy firefighters, Jake took her by the shoulders, and she swayed toward him. "Are you all right? I smelled gasoline as soon as I walked in there, but never expected a fire or an explosion."

"I'm all right, but I think my—" she looked down and held up one foot "—shoes melted or something."

He rubbed her arms. "If all you lost was a pair of shoes, this is your lucky day. What happened in there?"

"It was that box of rags." She shivered despite the warmth emanating from the fire and the cinders wafting through the air like fireflies.

Jake quirked his eyebrows. "Matt kept greasy rags in his storage unit for safekeeping?"

"The rags were wrapped around parts, motor-cycle parts. I don't know if the coverings started out clean, and gasoline and oil leaked onto them, or if Matt used purposely dirty rags to bundle the parts. I tipped the lid off the box to have a look inside, and it fell behind a carburetor or something, so I didn't put it back on right away, and the fumes escaped."

"And the fire just started automatically? You don't think he had something rigged up, do you?" His hands convulsively tightened on her arms.

"No, that was completely on me." She tapped her chest. "I did the stupidest thing imaginable. The light on my phone stopped working for some reason, and I was in the middle of going through the contents of another box. I—I had a lighter in my purse that I had picked up from Matt's apartment, and I flicked it on to see. I completely forgot about what was in the other box and how the fumes alone could ignite a fire."

"You used a lighter in a storage container with combustible auto parts?" Jake shook his head, trying to figure that one out. Sometimes smart people had no common sense.

"Stupid, I know." She wiped her hands along her grimy slacks. "Thanks for getting me out of there. I'm not sure I would've made it in time."

"I don't know." He slung an arm around her shoulders and pulled her close, because if she didn't welcome a hug after that escape, when would she? "That's the fastest I've ever seen anyone move backward in my life."

"Are you two okay?" A firefighter, his equipment squeaking, approached them.

"We're fine." Jake held out his hands. "Just a little singed hair and a few lungfuls of smoke."

"At least drink some water to soothe your throat. How'd that fire start?"

Kyra repeated her absurd story, which sounded even more ridiculous out loud in front of an incredulous firefighter.

He clicked his tongue. "Extremely dangerous. Is it you who stored those parts like that?"

"Me?" Jake pointed to himself. "No, sir. The contents of that container belonged to Ms. Chase's foster brother, now deceased."

"He didn't get the insurance. He didn't get the insurance." A small man with tufts of dark hair growing out of the side of his head scurried forward, waving papers. "That's Matt Dugan's unit, right? Number 556?"

"That's right. He passed away and left the contents— or what's left of them—to me." Kyra glanced at Jake quickly before returning her gaze to the storage facility's owner.

This was the first time Jake had heard of Matt's storage unit. Why hadn't Kyra told him? Instead, she'd hightailed it out of Quinn's place so fast he'd known something was up. Of course, her hasty departure could've meant she didn't want to spend time with him, but more than ego told him that wasn't the case.

He didn't want to get into that now. Her smoke-blackened face and glassy eyes told him not to go there…yet.

The owner took a wheezy breath. "I just want to let you know Mr. Dugan didn't have insurance on the unit. He declined it. I have the paperwork right here."

"That's okay, Mr.…?"

"Pargarian. Zev Pargarian."

"Mr. Pargarian. He really didn't have anything of value in there, anyway, unless you're into old motorcycle parts, I guess. And those are probably hot… stolen."

The firefighters had done their job, and Matt's unit crouched in its row, a smoking hulk of charred metal.

As the firefighters began to pack up their gear, the captain emerged from the ruins of Matt's life, carrying a box. "We were able to salvage one item.

This box was near the door and untouched when we arrived, so we moved it out of the way."

Standing beside him, Kyra stiffened and her body vibrated like a plucked violin string. "You saved a box?"

The captain placed it on the ground between Jake and Kyra, and she dropped her head to read the scribbling on the box's lid. Her body sagged. "I already went through that one. It's nothing but some papers and receipts. You can leave it, and Mr. Pargarian can trash it with the rest of the stuff when he does cleanup."

The captain shrugged in his giant moon suit and hauled the box back to the wreckage of the unit.

Jake opened his mouth and Kyra spun on him, holding out her hand. "I know you have questions, Jake. I have some for you, too, but can we save them until tomorrow? I'm exhausted and I want to drink some water or tea like the firefighter suggested. I'm hoping to salvage these slacks, too."

"Fair enough. You've had a shock. Can you drive home okay?"

"I'm fine. Thanks again for dragging me out of there." Her voice hitched, and she covered her mouth with her hand.

Was it an act to get out of explaining why she hadn't told him about the storage unit and crept off to investigate it on her own? Not that she didn't have every right to do that, as it belonged to her.

"I'm just glad I was there in time to help." He rubbed her back as he walked her to her car. "Take it easy, and drive carefully. I'll talk to you tomorrow."

He waved at her car as she drove away. The fire engines followed her out. Jake had left his own car on the street and had hopped the fence after following Kyra here. She'd never suspected a tail.

Jake wandered back to the debris from the fire and kicked a few of the auto parts, misshapen metal still smoldering. His gaze landed on the box Kyra had dismissed.

Had she really gotten a good look inside with the light from her cell phone? Maybe they were each looking for something different.

Bending at the knees, he hoisted the box into his arms and straightened to his full height. He could carry this without breaking a sweat.

He hugged the box to his chest as he swung by the front office. When Jake tapped on the door, Pargarian looked up from his desk and waved him in.

Jake dropped the box at his feet and pushed open the door that thousands of grimy hands had pushed before. He poked his head in the office and the scent of pine tickled his nose. "Can I ask you a couple of questions?"

Pargarian raised his bushy brows. "It's late and you burned down one of my units."

Jake took his badge from his pocket and flashed it. "Just a few questions. I won't take long, and technically Ms. Chase burned that baby down."

Pargarian plucked several tissues from a box and blew his nose while gesturing with his other hand for Jake to enter.

"Can you tell me the last time Matt Dugan visited his unit?"

"That's all?" Pargarian crumpled the tissues and dropped them in a wastebasket. Rubbing his hands together, he said, "I can tell you that."

Jake parked in front of the little man's desk as he tapped away on a keyboard. He leaned close to the screen and said, "Two months ago. The last time he entered the facility was just under two months ago."

Jake whistled. The papers in the box might not be so old after all.

Pargarian sat with his hands poised over the keys, looking like an incongruous receptionist. "Anything else? That was one question."

Jake jerked a thumb over his shoulder. "Not a question really. Just wanted to let you know I'm taking the one intact box from the fire. Ms. Chase didn't want it, but I'd like to have a look."

"She doesn't want it, and you're the cop. One less item for me to clean up."

Pargarian allowed him to walk out the front door of the office to exit the facility, and Jake hiked to his car, his arms wrapped around the box.

The whole event might turn into nothing at all, except for one thing. After they escaped the fire, Jake had watched Kyra take her phone from her purse and turn off the flashlight.

Either that flashlight came back on its own, or... she was lying and had set fire to the storage unit on purpose.

KYRA PEELED HER sooty slacks from her legs and tossed them in the corner of the bathroom. She didn't want to put them in the hamper with the rest of her dirty clothes and have everything smell like she'd been cleaning chimneys.

She hunched forward, her hands planted on the chipped tile of her vanity, and stared at her black-ringed eyes. She resembled some crazy raccoon, a feral creature who had acted out of instinct and fear.

While she hadn't realized setting the box of papers on fire would result in an explosion that could've killed her and Jake, it was a foolish, thoughtless act born of fear and desperation. She could've simply told Jake the boxes contained nothing of importance, hauled them away to her own place and set fire to the contents in a more reasonable way.

A laugh exploded from her chest, her smile a white gash across her black face. Reasonable? When had it become reasonable to set fire to papers? When had it become reasonable for acquaintances, coworkers, to follow you around the city and sneak up on you? She had a much better excuse for being at the storage unit alone than Jake had for creeping up on her there.

Although if he hadn't been playing detective, she might be part of Mr. Pargarian's cleanup about now. Jake had dragged her out of the unit when he could've turned and run. Everyone else in her life had always turned and run—everyone except Quinn and Charlotte. But Jake hadn't exactly been running toward *her*. He'd been running toward the storage unit.

Coughing more soot from her lungs, she shimmied

out of her underwear and bra. She added them to the heap of smoky clothes and whipped the mermaid-dotted shower curtain across the rod with a jangle. Cranking on the faucet, she stepped into the tub that doubled as a shower. Although everything in this apartment screamed 1980s, she'd be a fool to move and give up the rent control.

The warm water coursed over her head and down her face. She washed her hair and lathered up a sponge to scrub her body clean of the ashes and the smell of burnt hair.

After the shower, she dried her hair, slipped into a pair of gray sweats and a camisole, and bundled her clothes to take them to the laundry room later. She gargled with warm water and boiled a cup of hot water in the microwave.

As she curled up in front of the TV, swirling the tea bag around in the cup, the doorbell rang. Startled, she lost her grip on the tea bag and the little square of paper at the end floated to the top of the steaming liquid. She eyed her purse with her weapon still tucked in the side pocket. Who the hell was paying a visit at this time of night?

"Kyra, it's Jake."

She swallowed against her raw throat and walked to the front door. Hadn't they agreed to leave things for tomorrow? Lying got harder for her at the end of the day, harder when she'd shed her armor. Getting harder with Jake.

She twisted the dead bolt and cracked open the door as if she expected the Boston Strangler…or The

Player. Instead, Jake stood there with an uncertain smile on his handsome face and the box from Matt's unit in his arms. It wasn't *the* box, though.

She cleared her throat. "Is something wrong?"

"Gah." He grabbed his own throat. "I'm clearing my throat every five minutes. I found out something from Mr. Pargarian after you left, and I wanted to share it with you."

She blinked. He'd gone sleuthing behind her back?

Widening the door, she said, "You rescued that box of old papers? C'mon in."

He squeezed through, encased in the odor of the fire, hugging that damned box like it contained his last possessions on earth instead of Matt's.

"You smell." She pinched her nose. "I told you I went through that box. It contains some legal paperwork, receipts, nothing of importance."

"Maybe not." He tipped his chin toward the living room. "Can I set this down on the coffee table?"

"If you must." She wrinkled her nose.

"I know. I'm sorry. You smell like…roses." His face reddened as if he faced another fire. "Obviously, I came straight from the storage unit."

"I figured that." She crossed her arms over the thin white camisole, squishing down her braless breasts.

The previous and only time Jake had been in her apartment was when he had marched over here to confront her about being the daughter of one of The Player's victims. Now he was here to do what? Confront her about sneaking off to Matt's storage unit without telling him about it? She needed to do some confronting of her own.

She wedged her hands on her hips and thrust out her chest—to hell with her braless status. "I had every right to check out Matt's container on my own. I needed to do that by myself, and I don't appreciate that you tagged along."

He held up a pair of grimy hands. "I know. I could see something was off when you left Quinn's, and it's just the natural detective in me to want to find out the reason."

Her snort turned into a smile, and Jake jumped on it.

"Good excuse, huh?"

"It's just that—" she ran a hand through her loose hair "—Quinn always used to tell me that when I'd find him snooping through my things."

"Then I'm in good company." He started to sit down on her couch, and she waved her arms.

"I don't know if you've looked in the mirror, but you really are a mess. That T-shirt looks as if it's been used to fan a barbecue. I'd rather not have it on my couch."

"Sorry." Jake caught himself and tripped forward. "I can stand."

"Give it to me." She thrust out her hand. "I was just about to put my own clothes in the wash. I can add your T-shirt to the load."

He planted his hands against the thighs of his jeans. "As long as you don't take my jeans, too."

Tilting her head, she said, "They're not as bad

as the shirt. I'm surprised you had time to go home after work before going to Quinn's. You were even there early."

"Sometimes I keep a change of clothes in my locker at the station." He grabbed the hem of his T-shirt and pulled it over his head, and Kyra completely forgot what he'd just said.

She swallowed against her scratchy throat as she drank in Jake's hard slabs of muscle shifting across his chest, and the tighter washboard pattern that stamped his abs. She'd seen him in casual clothes before, so she knew he hid something…alluring beneath his button-up shirts and ties, but she hadn't realized he was sex on a stick, or rather a branch, a trunk.

"You have someplace you want me to put this?"

"Put what?" Her heavy eyes, sated with the pure masculinity of his body, slowly tracked to his face.

He waved the shirt in his hand like a white flag. "This T-shirt. Do you think it'll be done before I leave? I'd rather not drive home in my work car shirtless."

Home? She wasn't sure she wanted him to go home…ever.

"Yeah, yeah, I'll take it and dump it in with my stuff. The wash shouldn't take more than forty minutes, and the drying will be quick with just a few things in the dryer." She grabbed the shirt from his hand, careful to avoid the touch of his fingers. She'd almost been burned once tonight. She didn't need a scorching now.

Holding the shirt away from her body, she turned and looked back over her shoulder. "While I get our things in the laundry, you can wash up in the bathroom. I don't know what you used to clean your face after the fire, but it was largely ineffective. Then I'll get you some tea and honey for your throat and you can tell me what's so important about that box of junk."

"This way?" He pointed toward her bedroom door.

"There's a bathroom to your right." She didn't need the guy wandering through her bedroom, close to her bed.

She emptied the hamper in her bathroom and dumped the soot-stained clothes inside. Then she marched across the small courtyard to the laundry room and shoved everything into a washing machine.

When she returned to the apartment, she glanced briefly at Jake, hoping he hadn't removed any more of his clothing. With his jeans on below his bare torso, he perched on the edge of her couch, the lid now off the box and his hands plunged inside.

When would she finally get Matt out of her life for good? She banged around in the kitchen and held up a cup. "I'm going to make you some tea. One of the firefighters suggested tea and honey for the throat. Do you also want some water?"

He glanced up, his dark brows a V over his nose, both hands clutching pieces of paper. "Yeah, some water would be great."

She filled up a glass of water for him and took

it and her own teacup back into the living room. "What's so important about that box?"

"Besides the fact it's the only surviving item from Matt's storage container?" He took the glass from her hand and glugged down half the water, his eyes watering. "I needed that."

"I'll give you more once you start talking." She took a sip of tea, watching him through the steam.

He scooped up a handful of papers and waved it at her. "I don't know if you noticed when you looked in here the first time, but these are not all old. Pargarian told me that Matt had last been to the unit a couple of months ago—so, while the Copycat Player was still active and you were getting those playing cards."

"Okay." She hadn't noticed any dates. She'd been looking for more pictures and…evidence. "What's in there?"

"Like you said—legal papers, receipts, notes. But they're recent, from the time Matt was actively stalking you."

She shivered and cupped her tea. Judging from some of those photos in the box she'd torched, there hadn't been a time when Matt wasn't stalking her. "I'm not sure what you hope to find in there, Detective, but I'm willing to help you."

"Glad to hear that." He downed his water and held out his glass for more.

His tea had finished steeping, so she returned with his water in one hand and tea in the other. "After you rehydrate, you really should sip the tea. It helps."

"I will." He grabbed the edges of the box and

tipped it over on the coffee table. Stacks of clipped and stapled papers fell out, along with slips and scraps of paper.

She grabbed the ones bunched together and squinted at the embossed blue letterhead for an attorney's office. "I think we can sort these into Matt's legal documents, right?"

"You start that pile, and I'll fish out all the receipts. Who knows? They may be telling."

She'd figured Jake had used the box as an excuse to come over here and grill her about why she'd kept the storage facility a secret from him, but he barely touched on that and seemed to think they'd find something in this mess to support Matt's claim that someone had paid him to plant those cards near her apartment and car.

She had her doubts. Matt wasn't that organized. Most of his illegal dealings he kept in his brain, away from the prying eyes of the cops. Nobody could get into Matt's brain—at least not for free.

She stacked the documents in a neat pile detailing a very messy life.

She smoothed her hand over the stack. "Any luck?"

Jake looked up from the three piles he'd set up on the table. "No, but he has some purchases here I think his parole office would've been interested in knowing about."

"This is just wishful thinking. Even if you could find something that proved Matt took payment from someone to torment me with those cards, how would that help your case? Jordy is dead and gone."

"I feel it here." Jake pounded his bare chest with his fist. "It's an instinct. Ask Quinn."

"I've heard plenty about Quinn's instincts over the years. They didn't always pan out." She rose from her place on the floor across the coffee table from Jake. "More tea? Water?"

"The tea felt good on my throat, but I'll have some more water. Do you think the clothes can be switched to the dryer?"

"Probably close." She grabbed his glass and cup. "I'll check."

He curled his fingers around her wrist. "Do you take your piece with you when you go to the laundry room at night?"

"I don't usually do my laundry at night. I was going to save those sooty clothes for tomorrow."

Releasing her arm, he pushed off the couch, and a few of Matt's scraps showered to the floor. "Then let me go. Do you have any dryer sheets?"

"I already put one in the dryer next to the washer I used. Just load and go." She jingled a basket of coins on her way into the kitchen. "A quarter for ten minutes. You can probably get away with thirty. It's light stuff."

"I think I've got some change." He patted the front pocket of his jeans on his way out the door.

As she rinsed the two teacups, she mused on how great it was to have a half-naked man in her place doing laundry. She didn't know about his instincts, but she'd felt that he wanted to be close to her and just maybe it didn't have anything to do with Matt's bits of paper.

Jake yelled from the front door. "Hey, there's a mangy cat here trying to get in your apartment."

She leaned into the small foyer from the kitchen. "Keep him there. I'll bring him some milk and food."

She splashed a little milk into a bowl and took a box of kibble from the cupboard.

Jake widened the door for her, and the cat was threaded around his ankles. "I'm afraid to move."

"Good idea." She squeezed past him, and his bicep brushed the front of her camisole, giving her tingles in all the right places. She crouched, set down the milk and shook the dry food into the bowl already across from her door.

"You're an advocate for pets as well as people." Stepping back, he held the door open for her, giving her a wide berth.

Had he felt the electricity between them, too?

"Just this guy. The neighbors already hate me for encouraging him." She slipped back into the kitchen to get Jake more water.

He took up his position on the couch again, placing his glass on the end table. Rubbing his hands together, he said, "We're halfway through the box. I know Matt isn't going to disappoint."

"You don't know Matt." Before she sat, she reached across the table to grab the pieces of paper that had fallen to the floor. Jake had gotten the same idea at the same time, and they bumped heads.

"Ouch." She drew back, rubbing her forehead.

"Sorry." He reached across the coffee table and smoothed his thumb down her cheek. "You've had a rough night."

She parted her lips, unable to form one word. The rough pad of his finger felt like magic, soothing away any doubts she had about him. Her breath came out in short spurts, and her eyelashes fluttered as if she faced that inferno again and couldn't stare into the heat.

His thumb moved from her face to her bottom lip, which throbbed under his touch.

"You know—" his voice roughened as if he'd never had that tea "—we've never even kissed. I've thought about that a lot, wondered what your lips would taste like."

"And what did you come up with?" Her voice came out breathy like a bad actress in a B movie.

"Ice." His warm breath caressed her cheek, and she didn't even mind that it smelled slightly of charcoal. "A cool, cherry Popsicle."

"I think I'm going to disappoint you."

"Never." He slanted his mouth over hers and touched her lips in a light kiss. Then he deepened the kiss, caressing her lips with his own, his tongue probing in gentle exploration.

Her awkward position hunching over the coffee

table caused her to start listing to the side, so she curled an arm around Jake's neck to steady herself.

He took that as a definite yes and cinched his hands around her waist, pulling her toward him in another awkward scramble over the coffee table with Matt's life between them. That was no deterrent. She'd been waiting so long for the kiss that she could easily scale a coffee table.

Digging her fingers into Jake's broad shoulders, Kyra stepped over the table and fell against him. They toppled sideways onto the couch, and Jake, in a feat of grace and talent, never broke the connection of their kiss.

He moved his lips against hers. "Better to have you on my side."

As he rolled her onto her back, she splayed her hands across the hard planes of his chest. The man was solid in every way, and she wanted him on her side. She did.

He wedged his finger under her chin, tipping back her head. His kisses moved from scorching her lips to her jawline and then her neck.

Her head fell to the side as his tongue found the depression at the base of her throat. Her lashes fluttered open, and her clouded gaze swept the mess scattered across the table. She didn't want to think about Matt now. She didn't want to think about anything other than the sensations soaking her nerve endings.

Then a scribbled word jumped out at her from one

of the scraps of paper. She blinked and narrowed her eyes, even as Jake murmured a question in her ear, the low, throaty sound of an invitation.

She lifted her head, and her heart slammed against her chest as she made out the words: *laprey.*

Chapter Seven

Jake repeated the urgent question that had just left his lips, one hand splayed on the smooth skin of her stomach, his fingers inches from her right breast. "Do you want me to continue?"

Her body stiffened beneath his, and then her back arched, one leg slipping off the side of the couch. "Oh, my God."

He snatched his hand away from her warm belly. "I'm sorry."

She wriggled beneath him as if to dislodge him, and he sprang up and sat back on his heels.

Free of him, she scrambled from the couch, banging her shin on the coffee table and taking a few staggering steps like a boozer on a bender. Had he misread every sign from her?

"I'm sorry, Kyra. I thought…" He spread his hands, his naked torso making him feel exposed and clumsy.

Her fingers crept into her loose blond hair, and she shook her head back and forth. "You thought right. You did nothing wrong, Jake. It's me. I thought I was ready for something like this, and I'm just not."

Her words socked him in the gut, and he escaped from the soft couch that seemed to mock him now. "Yeah, sorry. I got carried away by the excitement of the evening. For a minute, I started believing I was the white knight who came to your rescue. My daughter keeps reminding me that girls don't need rescuing."

He was babbling like an idiot, and she looked as if she'd seen a ghost. His seduction techniques must've gotten really rusty in the years since his divorce.

"I'm sorry I intruded on your space. I'm sorry I came here unannounced."

She sliced her hand through the air. "Stop apologizing. I was all on board until…I wasn't."

"Okay. I'll get my shirt from the dryer and get out of your hair." His gaze wandered over her shiny tresses, free from the constricting ponytail for once. He'd been looking forward to running his own hands through those silky locks.

As he made a beeline for the front door, she called his name; he pretended not to hear. He was surprised he heard anything over the roaring in his ears. What an idiot. The woman was as cold as ice. She'd shown him that over and over. Shown him she couldn't be trusted.

He grabbed the hamper by the front door and stalked to the laundry room, feeling as if the fire from the storage facility had followed him. She'd lied to him tonight about going to the facility and then lied about the light on her phone dying. How many red flags did a man need?

He'd missed all the red flags his wife had been throwing about her affair, too. Maybe he was color-blind.

The dryer still had six minutes on the timer, but he stabbed the Cancel button anyway. He gritted his teeth as he watched the clothes flop around behind the glass door, mimicking his thoughts. He didn't even wait until the spinning stopped before he yanked open the door and thrust his hand into the warm drum.

He bunched the clothes in his fist and tossed them into the basket. He plucked his shirt from the pile and pulled it over his head. He'd be damned if he'd go back into that apartment half-naked, vulnerable.

Holding the hamper in front of him, he trudged back to her place. The green-eyed cat gave him a knowing look. "You know how it feels to be kicked out, too, don't you, buddy?"

He pushed through the door without even shutting it behind him and dropped the plastic hamper on the floor. "They're dry enough."

"Were you talking to someone out there?"

"The cat."

She had her hands in the pockets of her gray sweats, one bare foot on top of the other. "I'm sorry, Jake."

"Now we're both apologizing." He tugged on the hem of his shirt and smoothed out a wrinkle from the front. "Forget it. We both made a mistake."

Her eyes widened for a second, and the luscious

lips that had been his for such a short time trembled. "I…"

Pointing over her shoulder, he said, "I'm just gonna grab that stuff, if you don't mind. You said you didn't want the box."

"Oh, no, you can have it." She swept her arm to the side in a magnanimous gesture that seemed to promise the world instead of a box of junk. *You can't have me, but you're welcome to that crap.*

He walked past her, his back stiff. He placed the empty box on the floor at the edge of the table and swept everything inside it, destroying his careful sorting. It didn't matter. He had to get out of here.

He stopped at the door and glanced over his shoulder. "If your cough gets worse, see a doctor."

"You, too."

He raised his hand and escaped into the cool night, or maybe it just felt cool because of the heat bubbling inside him.

The cat flicked his tail and blinked. Jake growled at him. "Good luck."

WHEN JAKE SLAMMED the door, it seemed to shake the whole apartment—seemed to shake her to her bones. She dashed at the tear trailing down her cheek and withdrew the crumpled piece of paper from her pocket.

She didn't have time right now to regret her abrupt dismissal of Jake. She could've pretended. She could've put the paper's words, which matched the email address on the message, out of her head and made love to Jake. Matched him kiss for kiss. Still, if she was going to be with Jake, she wanted to give him her full attention. Now she might never have the chance at all.

She shook her head and smoothed the scrap of paper in her palm, reading it out loud. "'LA Prey' or 'La Prey.'"

What did it mean? Was it some Spanish word she didn't know? Didn't look Spanish. Or French. Could it be someone's name? Nobody would use their real name to send a threat to her.

But now she held a link in her hand that there was a connection between the cards left for her during Jordy Cannon's murder spree and the email sent to her after the murder of Andrea Miles. Matt had contact with La Prey. He was probably the one paying Matt to leave the playing cards. Now, with Matt gone, La Prey had taken on the job of tormenting her himself. Why?

She picked up Jake's glass from the end table with a stab of guilt piercing her heart. This was what Jake had been looking for—a strong suggestion that someone had paid Matt to plant the cards—and she'd hidden it from him. She'd done more than that to him, something she didn't want to examine right now.

Jake was wrong to believe her issues had anything to do with Jordy Lee Cannon's crimes or Andrea's murder. Finding out who was harassing her wasn't going to lead to Andrea's killer, and Jake had already dealt with Jordy.

Maybe Matt had been the one who was paying La

Prey, not the other way around. Matt had that picture of the foster family in his possession. He could've scanned it and sent it to La Prey to send on to her. Maybe Matt had already paid this guy to keep up the reign of terror against her. Maybe Matt's lackey didn't even know his benefactor was dead.

She put the cups in the dishwasher and picked up the hamper on the way to her bedroom. She plunged her hand into the warm, slightly damp clothes and dropped to the edge of the bed. Jake couldn't even wait for his T-shirt to dry—and she didn't blame him.

Why couldn't she just come clean with him... about everything? She fell back on the bed, her legs dangling over the side. And see *that* look in his eyes?

Was it worse than the look she'd witnessed tonight? Hurt? Confusion?

She rolled to her side, curling her legs to her chest. She needed to talk to someone. She needed her mom.

THE NEXT MORNING, Jake stumbled into the station, bleary-eyed and still hacking up black gunk. He'd inhaled more of that smoke than he'd thought—had made him go temporarily insane, too. From now on, Kyra Chase could stay in her corner and he'd stay in his.

He plopped into his chair and stared at his blank computer monitor. But, as long as he was in his corner, he had some work to do. He yanked open his top desk drawer and fished around for loose business cards, plucking them out one by one. He needed a better filing system.

A punch to his arm interrupted his task.

"What are you doing in there, searching for old lottery tickets?"

Jake jerked his head up at Billy and snapped his fingers in his face. "Weren't you dating someone from DCFS last year during one of your breaks with Simone?"

"Yes, I was." Billy rolled his eyes to the ceiling, finger on his chin. "Tara Liu."

"Did it end well?" Jake tapped a stack of business cards on his desk, holding his breath. You never knew with Billy.

"Yeah, yeah. Tara's a great girl. Bad timing all around." Billy folded his arms. "You need a favor?"

"Do you think Tara would be game?"

Billy winked. "She was game for a lot."

"Okay, I don't need to hear about it." Jake formed his fingers into a cross. "Do you think she'd help me out with something not by the book, as long as it wasn't hurting anyone?"

"As long as it doesn't hurt those kids. She's fiercely protective of the children in the system."

"This is old news, before her time. Do you have her direct number, and can I drop your name?" Jake swept the cards back into his drawer and slammed it. "Will she remember your name?"

"Really?" Billy tugged on the lapels of his expensive jacket.

"Okay, Romeo. Get me her number."

Billy pulled out his cell phone and tapped the screen. "I'll send it to you."

Seconds later, Jake's phone signaled a new message and he retrieved Tara Liu's number from Billy's text. He tipped the phone at Billy, who was slipping out of his jacket and taking the desk next to him. "Thanks."

Jake pushed the chair back, hand curled around his phone, and made for the door. He didn't need the whole task force listening in on every thread he decided to pursue—and he believed Matt Dugan's past was linked to these copycats.

He nearly plowed into Kyra at the entrance to the war room. "Whoa, sorry. How's your throat?"

"Still a little scratchy. Yours?"

"Same." He brushed past her, the phone digging into his sweaty palm. Without a backward glance, he took the stairs down to the first floor and burst out into the sunshine. He got behind the wheel of his Crown Vic and called Tara Liu.

Her impersonal voice-mail message greeted him. In her line of work, she probably didn't answer calls from unknown numbers, so he'd expected this.

"Tara, this is Detective Jake McAllister, LAPD Robbery-Homicide. I got your number from my partner, Billy Crouch. I have a favor to ask you…off the record."

She might not return his call due to that tagline, but he wanted to be up-front. He hated the gradual wheedling of favors from people, the groveling and begging. He liked to state his case and know right away if it was a go.

He dragged a sheet of paper from his pants pocket

containing information about Matt Dugan's time in the system and smoothed it out on his thigh.

The phone rattled in his cup holder, and he grabbed it, seeing Tara's number on the display. "McAllister."

"Detective, this is Tara Liu with DCFS returning your call."

"Thanks for the speedy response, Tara, and you can call me Jake."

"Not J-Mac?"

"If you want. I take it Billy told you some stories about me—all false, I'm sure."

Her laugh trilled over the line. "How is Billy? Back with his wife?"

Jake swallowed, not wanting to get caught up in Billy's tangled romantic web. "On and off. You know."

"I *do* know." She cleared her throat in a way that marked a delineation between social and business. "What can I help you with? Are you and Billy on the Andrea Miles case?"

"We are. We re-formed the task force and are treating this like a possible serial."

She sucked in a breath. "You want my help with that?"

"It is related." He thought so, anyway. He didn't have to give her all the details. Her voice indicated she'd be eager to help with a serial killer case.

"I can help you off the record, but not if it puts any of my kids at risk. Is that understood?"

"Yes, ma'am." He folded the corner of the paper in his lap and took a deep breath. "I'm looking for information about a person who left the system about ten years ago. You weren't with the department then, were you?"

"Just a grad student in social work, but I can access the records. What are you looking for?"

"Primarily the names of his foster families while he was in the system, when he was a teen. I don't need the whole history."

During the silence on the other end of the line, Jake chewed on his bottom lip.

"The families are supposed to have anonymity." Tara clicked her tongue. "But you are a cop, and you're working a case. I can get you that info on your subject, and it doesn't even have to be under the radar. I wouldn't be doing anything sneaky."

"I don't want to have to go through regular channels, Tara. I don't want to do the paperwork or have to come up with a subpoena. Are you down with that?"

Her answer came almost immediately. "I don't know why, but I know enough from dating Billy that you guys do things off the record for a reason."

Jake gave a silent thanks to his partner and let out a quiet breath through his nostrils. He didn't want to let on to Tara that he'd been holding it. "Thanks. I'll be in your debt, so if you ever need anything, don't hesitate to ask."

"Ooh, I like the sound of that—not that Billy isn't already in my debt, but to have two LAPD homicide detectives at my beck and call is delicious."

Again, the clearing of the throat to return to business. "What's the name of this person?"

Jake crumpled the piece of paper with Matt's info on it. He didn't owe anything to Kyra. If she was going to play games with him, he'd play.

"The name of the person is Lake. Marilyn Lake."

"Oh, I thought you were going to give me a male name."

So did I.

He answered, "Did you? You must've misunderstood or I misspoke. This is a girl I'm tracking."

"Marilyn Lake. Left the system about ten years ago?"

"Yes."

"Middle name?"

"Monroe, if you can believe that, and her nickname was Mimi."

"I don't laugh at anyone's names. My name is Tara Scarlett, and I'm Chinese." She shuffled some papers, or maybe that was chewing. "I will look into Marilyn Monroe Lake, and I'll get back to you later today if I have the time. Is there a deadline on this?"

"Today would be great if you can get to it, but there's no urgency."

When the call ended, Jake sat in his car cupping his phone in his hands. The conversation with Tara had left a bad taste in his mouth, and he had to work hard to convince himself he wasn't doing this as revenge for getting shut down by Kyra.

Kyra was keeping something from him that he believed could help in this investigation. He had to

trust that she didn't think her information was rel-
evant. He couldn't see her allowing a killer to roam
free if she really thought she had a way to stop him.

Nonetheless, she wasn't a detective.

He'd been planning to ask Tara to research Matt,
but if Matt and Kyra had shared the same foster family at one point, he might as well start with Kyra's
background—and that picture she took from Matt's
dresser mirror.

Jake swung one leg out of the car and planted it
on the ground. Though his phone had been going off
while he'd been on the line with Tara, he didn't plan
on making this car his permanent office. He'd return
the calls when he got back to his desk.

As he got out of the car, Billy rushed toward him,
pointing a finger at his chest. "You're already in position, so you can drive."

Jake's pulse jumped. "Drive where?"

"There's been another homicide. Our killer just
gave us another chance to catch him."

Chapter Eight

Jake peeled off his gloves and shoved them into the pocket of his jacket. He flipped his sunglasses over his eyes and peered at Billy pacing the sidewalk in front of Crystal Monroe's house, occasionally shouting instructions at some poor cop who got into his line of sight. His partner needed to talk to Kyra.

Jake pulled back his shoulders and strode toward Billy. "I think we can let the CSI guys do their thing, Cool Breeze."

Billy's nickname had never fit him less.

He ran a hand through his short Afro, a muscle ticking wildly at the corner of his mouth. "Coroner's van isn't here yet. We could've missed something. I need to take another look at her, one more look at her hair."

Jake grabbed Billy's sleeve as he turned toward the house. "That's Crystal Monroe, brother. She's not Sabrina, any more than Andrea was."

"But her hair, Jake." Billy's dark, liquid eyes pleaded with him. "There's something about her hair."

Jake released Billy's arm and patted it, while swiveling his head around. Nobody needed to see Billy falling apart at the scene of a homicide.

"Sure, man. Let's have another look at her hair." He wiggled his fingers into another pair of gloves as he followed Billy back into the house and then the bedroom, where the body of Crystal lay tucked up in her bed.

Poking his head into the room, Jake said, "Can I get you ladies and gents to clear out for a minute? One more thing we need to check on the body."

The crime scene techs grumbled as they packed away their equipment, and Clive, who was just about to dust for prints on the closet door, raised his eyebrows at Jake.

Jake gave Clive a slight shrug and pulled the door closed after him. "Billy, you need to get it together. This is his second African American victim, but it doesn't mean he's specifically targeting Black women, and they have nothing to do with…"

Billy raised a hand. "Sabrina used to do her hair like this sometimes, but Crystal's looks uneven."

Jake turned his gaze to the pretty young woman with her curly hair dancing on her shoulders, the queen of diamonds between her lips and a stain on her yellow bedspread where her left hand lay, bereft of its pinkie finger.

"Okay, Billy, check out her hair. Do your thing."

Billy reached out a trembling hand and took a lock of Crystal's hair between his gloved fingers. He pulled it out straight to its full length. Keeping the hair extended, he repeated the process with the other side like a hairdresser checking for symmetry. It didn't reach as far as the other lock of hair.

Billy twisted his head over his shoulder, a triumphant light in his eyes, a lift to the corner of his mouth. He whispered, "He took it. He snipped off some of her hair to keep for himself."

And bam—Billy had discovered the personal trophy for this killer, the one Quinn insisted had to exist to give the murders meaning beyond the copycat aspect.

"Good job." Jake thumped Billy on the back. "Now let's allow the techs back in here before they riot."

As they walked to the car, Billy's shoulders started to slump, and he was almost doubled over by the time Jake stuffed him into the passenger seat. He turned to Billy.

"These women have nothing to do with your sister, Billy. Sabrina is not going to all of a sudden turn up a victim of this killer."

"Maybe not *this* killer." Billy slammed his fist against the dashboard. "I'm sorry, Jake. I don't know what came over me when I saw Crystal dead and realized we had a second Black victim. It's not that it's any more horrendous because this killer is targeting African American females. That's not what has me upset."

Jake clapped Billy on the shoulder. "I know that. You're thinking about Sabrina. You're seeing your sister in these victims. It's bringing back her disappearance all over again."

Billy covered his eyes briefly. "Did I make a fool of myself back there?"

"I don't think anyone other than me noticed you weren't being Cool Breeze. However—" Jake started the engine "—we do have a therapist on the task force. Take advantage of that. Kyra's here to help not just the victims' families but the cops on the task force."

"Is she helping you?" Billy's sly smile indicated he was coming back to himself.

"I think we're probably better off as colleagues."

"If you say so." Billy grabbed the door handle.

"Where are you going?" Jake asked.

"We have to finish canvassing the neighborhood. I'm sure there are more than a few cameras around. No visible signs of break-in, victim murdered in bed. He was lying in wait for her, just like with Andrea. He knew her habits, knew she lived alone. He must've been stalking her."

"Are you all right? I can do it. You can take the car back to the station, and I'll catch a ride with one of the patrol units."

"Really?" Billy tipped his sunglasses to the edge of his nose. "We all know I'm the charming one. How are you going to get those neighbors to talk?"

Jake swallowed the lump in his throat. "Good to have you back."

He and Billy spent the next two hours going door-to-door, viewing and, in some cases, taking video footage from home security systems.

If Crystal had a stalker, they were going to find him.

JAKE AND BILLY burst into the task force war room, their shoulders thrust back in confidence, their heads held high with bravado. Her heart flipped. Had they found something?

Would Jake mention anything outside the task force briefing? He hadn't bothered to tell her there had been another murder. She'd found out just like everyone else at the station.

Her jaw hardened. If she'd put out last night for Jake, would she still be in his cozy confidence?

Her eyes stung, and she blinked. That wasn't fair to Jake. He'd been reading all her signs correctly until she saw that slip of paper. Now he wanted to get things back on a professional level to protect himself. She got that.

She shoved away from her desk and marched up to the two detectives. "You guys look like you found something."

"We think he stalked this victim, too." Billy's gaze darted from Jake's face to hers. "We're going to compare some of the cars coming and going in Crystal's neighborhood to the ones in Andrea's neighborhood."

"I can start that." Jake shoved Billy toward Kyra. "Why don't you take our resident therapist out for lunch."

"Me?" Kyra poked a finger at her chest. "Things not going well with Megan? You need another setup?"

"Ooh, savage." Billy clutched his chest and fake-stumbled back. "Actually, I'd like to…get a few things off my chest, and Jake suggested I talk to you."

He did? Her skin tingled. She must not be completely on his blacklist.

"Then lunch it is. Come get me when you're ready. I'm going to reach out to Crystal's family." She sauntered back to her desk, and twenty minutes later Billy approached her, his usual swagger subdued.

"I'll drive, and I have a place in mind, if that's okay."

"Lead the way." She grabbed her sweater and purse from the back of her chair. Even in a mood, Billy displayed his chivalry by stopping at the door and sweeping her through with his arm.

He led her to his sedan, and twenty minutes later they were seated in a booth in a dark Italian restaurant more suited to an illicit afternoon affair than a conversation about murder...although Kyra had a feeling they weren't here to discuss the Copycat Player case, at least not directly.

Billy got down to business after they both ordered chopped salads and iced teas. Hunching over the table, elbows planted on either side of the basket of garlic bread, Billy rested his chin on his folded hands. "I had a...a kind of breakdown this morning at Crystal's murder scene."

She schooled her face into a smooth palette. Billy had been around the homicide block several times, and a strangulation did not usually present the most gruesome of murder scenes. Had he hit a wall this time?

As the thoughts careened through her brain, pinging off each other, she simply said, "Go on."

"Crystal was a young African American woman, like Andrea Miles. And like I told Jake, the fact that the victims are Black or that this killer may be targeting Black women doesn't make it worse because I'm also Black." He ran a hand over his mouth. "But it does make it worse for me because my sister Sabrina disappeared five years ago."

"I'm sorry."

"Poof." He snapped his fingers. "She was gone without a trace. Took her keys, her phone, her car and then disappeared off the face of the earth."

Although Kyra had many questions about Sabrina's disappearance, that was not why they were here. "Seeing these murdered women makes you think about Sabrina."

"Yes, and it's crazy because neither of them particularly looked like my sister and Sabrina wasn't assaulted or taken from her home. Her car, with her purse, her turned-off phone, her keys, was found abandoned at a store near the airport. No sign of foul play. So, it's not like I believe Sabrina could've been a victim of this same killer five years ago. It's just seeing these lifeless women reminds me of my sister."

"Did you have the same feelings of panic when you saw Andrea's body, too, or just today?"

"I felt—" he picked up a piece of garlic bread with his long fingers and ripped it apart "—strange when I saw Andrea's body. Sad. I mean—don't get me wrong—we always feel sad, bad, upset for the victims. We're human, but we have a job to do there, and I've always been able to do that job dispassionately because that's the best way to respond to get justice for these victims."

She nodded, and he dropped the mangled bread on his plate. "I don't know why I'm telling you that. You're good friends with Roger Quinn, one of the most legendary detectives LAPD has ever seen. I'm sure you know how we operate."

"I want to know how *you* operate." She tipped her head at the approaching waiter, who seemed well versed in discretion.

"Not like this." Billy stabbed at his salad, spearing a pepperoncini. "How do you think I got my nickname?"

She cocked her head, taking in his tailored shirt, a pale yellow she was pretty sure only he could pull off with the turquoise tie. "Jake assured me it was your sartorial splendor."

Billy's familiar grin broke for the first time since she had seen him at the station. "That's part of it, but I tend to keep a cool head during investigations. J-Mac is the hothead, but then you already know that."

"We're here to talk about you." She poked around her salad. "Why do you think you started losing your... cool over Andrea's murder?"

He set down his fork and gazed into his tea. "Maybe it's the time of year. Summer to fall. There's always a stillness to the air in LA about now. Do you feel it? It was like this when Sabrina went missing."

She did feel it. The Player had murdered her mother about the same time of year. In fact, that anniversary was approaching.

Nodding, her mouth full, Kyra allowed Billy to set up the scene. She'd prefer he discuss his feelings, but he was a detective and narrative trumped feelings. He recited the events with no emotion, as if they'd been running through his head on a constant loop. They probably had been.

"Sabrina was the youngest of my three sisters, sort of an afterthought. She was just twenty when she disappeared." His hand fisted around his fork. "It's not even classified as a homicide, even after all these years, because there was no evidence she didn't leave voluntarily. I knew she hadn't, though. She wouldn't. She was in school, working, had a social life."

Kyra asked, "You were a detective at that time?"

"Yeah, that's the crazy part. It was my job, and I couldn't find her."

"Did she disappear in the Northeast Division?"

He swallowed. "No. She was living in Riverside at the time."

"So, finding her really wasn't your job, was it?" She swirled the ice in her glass with a straw. "But finding this second copycat, the one who murdered these two African American women, *is* your job."

"We have to get him, Kyra. We can't let him get away with this. Those families need justice. Hell, all

families need justice. Those women need justice…
and so does Sabrina."

"You've brought justice to a lot of families, Billy,
yet all that can't make up for your failure to find Sabrina."

He choked on a leaf of lettuce and covered the
lower half of his face with a napkin. "You just told
me it's not my fault, not my failure."

"You don't believe that."

"I don't." He crumpled the napkin on the table,
keeping it in his hand. "Do you think if we catch this
guy, I can forgive myself? Maybe come to believe
Sabrina's disappearance isn't my fault?"

"I don't know, Billy." Had she ever forgiven herself for sleeping through her mother's murder? The
cops never caught The Player. Quinn couldn't catch
him. Her mother never got justice.

She sipped her iced tea and met Billy's anxious
expression over her straw. "Tell me how you felt
when you saw Crystal's body in that bed."

Jake unwrapped his Italian sub and took a bite. As he
mopped the oil dribbling down his chin, he glanced
toward Kyra's corner desk. She and Billy had been
gone for over an hour. If anyone could help his partner, Kyra could.

Jake had tried to do some digging on his own into
Sabrina's disappearance and kept coming up against
a brick wall. Her car, purse and phone had been found
in a big-box store parking lot, out of the camera's

sight. There had been no sign of a struggle, but Sabrina had never used a debit or credit card again.

She'd dropped off the face of the earth. The original detectives on the case had few leads—no boyfriend, no ex-husband, no jealous women, not even a possible serial killer operating in the area of Riverside at the time.

Didn't mean there wasn't one. Didn't mean some guy wasn't traveling from state to state snatching women. Not all serial killers had a hunting ground or even an MO or signature.

The Player had changed up his MO from dumping his victims to strangling them in their homes to murdering them in their cars and leaving them. Serial killers could change their MOs but rarely changed their signatures. The Player's signature had been the card in the mouth and the missing finger.

And his disciples were copying his signature. Why? Why now? Disciples?

His cell phone rang and his heart thumped when he saw Tara Liu's number. She worked fast. It wasn't even the end of the day.

He got up from his desk and meandered to the window. "Hey, Tara. What did you find?"

"I found something quite interesting, Jake."

A soft rustle filled the pause and he couldn't stand it a second longer. "What?"

"I found nothing at all for Marilyn—Mimi—Lake."

"That's not possible. I know she was in the system."

"Oh, she's in the system, all right. I just can't access any of her files."

"What does that mean?"

"Marilyn Lake's DCFS files are on permanent lockdown. I don't think the Pope himself could get in there."

Chapter Nine

"Next time it's on me."

Jake's head jerked up at the sound of Kyra's voice floating across the room. He turned to the side and practically whispered into the phone. "Tara, do me one more favor. Check Matt Dugan's records for about the same time. Gotta go. Thanks."

Jake ended the call as Billy sauntered to the desk next to his. His partner shrugged out of his jacket and hung it over the back of his chair. He sat forward on the chair so as not to wrinkle his threads and peered over the top of his monitor.

Watching Kyra talk to Brandon, their tech guy, Billy spoke out of the side of his mouth. "That was a good call, man. Spilling my guts to Kyra helped. I promise I'm not going to fall apart at the next crime scene, regardless of whether or not the victim looks like my sister."

"Nothing to be ashamed about, Billy." With Kyra in his sights, Jake narrowed his eyes. "Did she do some voodoo on you? Hypnotize you? Put you into a trance?"

Billy cocked his head. "No, man. We just talked. In fact, she didn't say much at all. I know you don't put much stock in therapy, but there's something about it that helps."

"I'm glad. That's why I suggested it." Jake smacked his hand on the desk. "Now that she shrunk your head, we can get back to it."

"Did you go through the footage from the security cameras around the neighborhood?" Billy scooted his chair closer to Jake's desk and stared at the frozen video on Jake's computer screen.

Jake jabbed his fingers at the screen, circling a dark SUV. "We've already started identifying some of the cars that have repeat appearances on the block, and we've ruled out several as belonging to Crystal's neighbors. We also haven't noticed any vehicles that were present near both Andrea's and Crystal's houses."

Billy scratched his chin. "He could've driven two different cars. He's gotta know we're sitting here scanning security systems."

"Oh, he knows, all right." Jake shifted his mouse around and clicked on a couple of different icons on his display. "One security system on the block has been on the fritz the past few weeks. Guess which one."

"The one across the street from Crystal's. The one that would've had a clear view of her garage."

Jake snapped his fingers and pointed at Billy. "Bingo."

Billy whistled through his teeth. "The killer disabled it?"

"Most likely, isn't it? I mean, are we really supposed to believe that the most crucial camera is the one that's out?"

"What about in Andrea's neighborhood? Same thing?" Billy's dark eyes shone with curiosity and excitement, and Jake silently thanked Kyra for bringing his partner back, even though her own life remained shrouded in mystery.

"Perfect timing on that question. I was just about to look at some files Brandon sent me right before you and Kyra came back. Some of the homeowners on Andrea's block weren't around when the guys stopped by to collect video. They did another sweep, and Brandon sent me the results."

As Jake selected the different files, Billy hung over the keyboard, his breath coming in quick spurts. Jake waved the air in front of Billy's face. "Dude, lay off the garlic for lunch."

Grinning, Billy nodded toward Kyra, still in deep discussion with Brandon. "Then you'd better not kiss Ms. Chase over there. She ate the same thing I did for lunch."

Kiss Kyra? He'd be lucky if he got even that from her after she'd stopped his advances cold. And if she found out he was digging into her past, it would probably be game over.

"Okay, I'll remember that. In the meantime—" he flipped his hand in Billy's face "—back off."

Billy repositioned himself until he launched forward, bathing the air in enough garlic to ward off a bunch of vampires. He poked his finger at one of the files. "That's the address across from Andrea's house."

Jake opened the file, and they both slumped back in their chairs. Jake announced the bad news for both of them. "No security system at that house."

Billy said, "The next file must be the house next to it, but still across and in view of Andrea's garage."

Jake double clicked on the next file and choked when it opened.

This time Billy did the honors. "Damn, a security system that's been disabled for a few weeks. I know these things have issues—God knows we've had our problems with store and gas station footage—but what are the chances that security systems in two different locations, just where we need them, are down?"

"Without someone tinkering with the cameras, I'd say chances are pretty low." Jake crossed his hands behind his head and laced his fingers. "Our guy's not stupid. He's aware of the technology and he's savvy enough to disable it."

Billy drummed his long fingers on the desk. "Savvy enough to disable it and avoid it. We're not going to see his car on Andrea's or Crystal's streets. But we might…"

And like a good partner, Jake finished Billy's thought. "See it on another street. He may have crept into their neighborhoods on foot to avoid detection, but he had to have gotten there somehow. He wouldn't use public transportation with all the cameras and witnesses."

"I will set up a canvassing of the surrounding

streets and see if we can pull some more video."
Billy pushed back his chair.

"Brush your teeth first, seriously." Jake's phone
buzzed on his desk, and his nosy partner glanced at
the display.

"You reached Tara, huh?" Billy winked. "Give
her my regards."

"Excuse me."

Jake nearly jumped out of his chair at the sound of
Kyra's voice. She glided around here too silently for
his liking. He nervously covered his buzzing phone
with his hand.

"I'm sorry. You can get that." She pointed to the
phone he was foolishly trying to hide.

"I'll call back." He raised his eyebrows and pasted
on a fake pleasant smile—or at least he thought it
was pleasant. He usually didn't do pleasant. "What
can I help you with?"

What can I help you with? That sounded fake
as hell.

She tilted her head slightly, her blond ponytail
slipping over her shoulder. She'd had her hair loose
the other night, and his fingers tingled with the memory of weaving them through her silky strands.

A rosy pink edged into her cheeks, but her blue eyes
had a steely look. "Sorry to interrupt. I just wanted
to let you know that the victims' advocacy group I'm
working with is sending a car to the airport to meet
Andrea's parents. I'm going to be there."

"Thanks for letting me know." Jake slid his hand

from his phone and turned it facedown on his desk. "Those poor people."

"If they let slip any pertinent information about Andrea, I'll let you know so you can bring it up when you question them."

"Thanks, Kyra...and thanks." He jerked his thumb at Billy, now on the phone organizing the video collection effort around the two victims' homes.

"He'll be fine, but he needs to find his sister. Now I'll let you get back to your call." She drilled her index finger into the back of his phone and then spun around.

He released a long breath and scooped up the phone once Kyra had left the war room. Turning his back on Billy, he called Tara. "You have something for me on Matt Dugan already?"

"He was easier and I was already in the database, but don't get too excited."

Jake's leg started bouncing beneath the desk. "His files are locked down, too?"

"Not quite. I can see when he entered the system and his first several foster homes, but his record goes dark at about the time you're requesting. In other words, I can't access information about his final foster family before he was released from the system."

"Because it was Kyra's family."

"What?"

"Never mind. Thanks for your help, Tara. I owe you one, and I mean it."

"Don't you worry. I'll collect someday when you least expect it."

Jake ended the call and stared at Kyra's empty desk. Why were her and Matt's DCFS files hush-hush? He doubted the Pope had anything to do with the lockdown, but Kyra had some powerful people in her corner.

If the blackout was for her benefit... Maybe he'd had it all wrong. Maybe Kyra didn't even know about the secrecy of her DCFS files.

He had no intention of stopping here. What kind of detective would he be if he did? His gaze surveyed the room and locked onto Captain Castillo. If Kyra had powerful allies, Jake would start with one up close and personal.

KYRA STOOD BESIDE her car, pretending to look at her phone, keeping one eye on Billy's Crown Vic. If he was going to check out the cameras in the vicinity near the victims' homes, he'd have to take a trip out there—and she'd wait for him for however long it took.

It didn't take long.

With his tailored jacket draped over one arm, Billy strode to his car, his step faltering when he saw her.

She waved and called out, "Getting some directions. On your way to check out security systems?"

He drew closer and answered, "I am. That SOB had to get to those houses some way, even if he did jump over a few fences to conceal his arrival."

She clicked her remote and turned suddenly as if

she'd just thought of something. "Do I have to worry about Tara?"

"Huh?" Billy tilted his head down and peered at her over the top of his designer sunglasses.

"Tara, the woman calling Jake." She dropped her head and scuffed the toe of her shoe against her tire. "Is she my rival?"

Billy threw his head back and laughed. "An emphatic no on that one. Jake barely has time to handle one woman, let alone two. You're in the clear."

"Whew." She flicked her fingers across the nonexistent sweat on her forehead. "You said you knew Tara. Just a work thing?"

"Someone I dated at DCFS. Jake was looking for a favor." Starting for his car, Billy called over his shoulder, "I'll let him know you were worried. He'd be flattered."

"Oh, God. Please don't embarrass me. I'll look like a jealous idiot."

Billy lifted his hand, threw open his car door and got inside.

She sure hoped that was a sign of agreement. If Billy mentioned this conversation to Jake, he'd know that she knew he was looking into her background. It had to be that…didn't it?

She dropped behind the wheel of her own car and clutched it with both hands. Maybe she was being paranoid. Detectives often worked with DCFS. Why wouldn't Jake want a favor from one of the caseworkers?

Why should he hide his phone from her? Not that

she hadn't been known to get nosy and try to see who was texting him. If she hadn't been snooping, she never would've learned about his meeting with Matt.

Why did he have to go behind her back? She bit the inside of her mouth, drawing blood. He went behind her back because she lied to him at every turn—and at every turn he met her at the pass.

Sighing, she cranked on the engine of her car. Although she'd been deceiving people all her life, she'd never tried it on a detective before. Quinn knew all her secrets. Hell, Quinn knew her secrets better than she did.

Quinn had told her to trust Jake, tell him everything. Easy for Quinn to say. She could do no wrong in Quinn's eyes. Ever since he'd rescued her, covered in her own mother's blood, stiff with shock and fear, he'd protected her. She walked on water, as far as Quinn was concerned; Jake had different standards.

Jake's wife had cheated on him, and as much as he blamed himself for her infidelity, he would never be able to trust a woman whose whole life was one big deception—a woman like her.

She flexed her fingers on the steering wheel of the car and set out to meet the other victims' rights advocate who'd be meeting Andrea's parents at the airport with her. Her breathing had returned to normal and her heart beat in her chest at a steady pace.

She didn't like that Jake was possibly snooping around in her background, but she knew he wouldn't find what he was looking for.

Her DCFS files were protected more securely than the gold in Fort Knox.

JAKE HUNG ON Castillo's door frame. "Can I talk to you for a minute, Captain?"

The captain glanced up, a quick look of irritation on his haggard face. By Castillo's appearance, you'd think he was the one in charge of a task force for a serial killer who'd just claimed his second victim.

Castillo recovered quickly. "Sure, sure. Sit down. I heard Cool Breeze is out there casting a wider net for security footage. Good idea."

Jake closed the door behind him and sat in one of the chairs facing Castillo's neat desk, his gaze tracking across the family pictures behind Castillo's head— soccer games, ballet recitals, vacations to Yellowstone. He'd missed out on all that with his own daughter.

"We discovered two cameras facing the victims' houses that weren't working in the crucial weeks leading up to their murders. We think he disabled them somehow."

Castillo tapped his pen on the desk blotter. "It doesn't sound like we're dealing with a stupid killer here, does it? Jordy Lee Cannon made the mistake of having prior contact with his victims. This guy seems to be choosing his randomly—unless he's zeroing in on African American women. You think the killer could be Black? Rare for a serial killer."

"It is, although not unheard-of. We did have the Grim Sleeper, who operated for years."

"How's Billy holding up?"

Jake's eyes popped open for a split second. Had the uniforms been talking? "He's great, good. Sharp as ever."

"Okay." A smile hovered at Castillo's lips. He knew Jake would never betray his partner. "You had a question about the task force? Need more people?"

"I had a question about Kyra Chase."

Castillo's eyes blinked rapidly. His hands rearranged items on his desk as if mimicking the sorting going on in his brain. "I thought you were happy with her help on the Copycat Player task force. Is there a problem now? You have to let go of that incident with Lizbeth Kruger, Jake."

Jake's blood percolated as he sliced his hand through the air. "It has nothing to do with that, and I'm not ever going to get over that betrayal, but I've put it behind me."

"Then what about Kyra?"

"I, uh, stumbled across her files in DCFS." Jake rubbed out a spot on the edge of Castillo's desk with the pad of his thumb. "They're blocked, blacked-out, whatever you want to call it."

Castillo's dark eyebrows, where the salt hadn't invaded the pepper yet, jumped, and a look Jake couldn't identify spasmed across his face. "Why would you be looking into Kyra's foster system files?"

"I wasn't specifically looking into them." The lie slid from his mouth even as he knew that Castillo knew he was lying. "Just stumbled across. I was surprised they were locked down. Did Detective Quinn order that?"

Castillo spread his hands. "I have no idea. Didn't know they were dark, wouldn't know why they were dark, and, frankly, I don't care. I've heard some rumors that you and Kyra are...close. If you're using department resources to conduct your own background investigation on a romantic interest, I don't have to tell you how that looks—even if you are J-Mac, the hotshot homicide detective. Got it? Stop looking."

Jake's hands curled into fists on his knees. He didn't like Castillo's tone or his implications, but the captain wasn't wrong. He splayed his fingers and took a deep breath. He'd come a long way in his anger-management techniques.

"Understood. That's not the reason, by the way, but understood anyway. It has more to do with her foster brother Matt Dugan. I'll back off."

"Dugan has a rap sheet a mile long. All you have to do is look at it to follow the course of his sorry life." Castillo placed his hand on the receiver of his phone. "If there's nothing else, McAllister, I have a few calls to make before I leave today."

"Thanks for your time, Captain." Jake heaved himself out of the comfortable chair and shut Castillo's door behind him...very softly. Didn't want to give the guy the wrong impression.

Why the hell was Castillo so adamant about Jake keeping his hands off Kyra's files? Was the captain somehow involved in the masking?

By the time Jake returned to the task force conference room, most of his team members had left for the day. He sat heavily at his desk and rubbed his eyes.

Although he should just leave Kyra to her secrets, he couldn't shake the feeling that Kyra's past was somehow linked to these copycat killings. The obvious flag for his hunch was that her mother had been one of The Player's victims twenty years ago. As well, the lead homicide investigator on the case had taken Kyra under his wing. To the point where he'd ordered her DCFS record sealed?

Jake would bet on that. No use asking the old detective about it. Quinn's loyalty toward Kyra ran deep and wide. He'd never betray her secrets.

Jake rubbed his chin. Even if that betrayal meant catching a serial killer? But did it? What proof did he have that Kyra's background, other than the murder of her mother, had anything to do with the current rash of killings?

He grunted softly to himself. Maybe he should just be honest with himself and admit that he wanted to learn everything there was to know about Kyra Chase because he wanted…Kyra Chase.

He felt an undeniable connection and attraction to her despite the secrets that had erected a barrier between them. The roadblock wasn't just on his side, either. After his marriage crashed and burned, he vowed to never get into a relationship with a woman he couldn't trust.

Still, Kyra had her own reasons for holding him at

arm's length. She didn't trust him, either, or at least she didn't trust him with her secrets.

Maybe she was right. Despite the strong chemistry between them, they weren't meant to be. Even if the attraction was good enough for a roll in the sheets a few times, at this point in his life he wanted more than that. He had a daughter he hardly knew. He wanted to establish some kind of home life here in LA, an environment where Fiona could visit more frequently.

He logged off his computer and shoved it into his case, along with files and notes on Andrea and Crystal. A folder fell on the floor, spilling its contents, and he looked into the dead eyes of Andrea Miles.

As he shoved the photo back into the folder, he muttered to himself, "Great environment for Fiona."

He slung his bag over his shoulder and swept his phone off the desk. It buzzed in his hand, indicating a text message. Maybe Billy had already gotten a line on some video.

Cupping the phone in his hand, he glanced at the display—unknown number, not uncommon for his work phone. He perched on the edge of his desk and opened the text: Buck and Lori Harmon are the names you're looking for.

Jake cocked his head and reread the message. Was he looking for names? He texted back: Who is this?

The message showed that it was delivered. He stared at his phone for two minutes. Then he called back the number. It went straight to a recording informing him that there was no voice mail for the number.

Someone wanted to remain anonymous. He'd never heard of Buck or Lori Harmon and didn't know he was looking for them.

One of the officers they'd brought onto the task force to help survey video called from across the room. "J-Mac, I'm out for the duration. You're the last man standing. You wanna lock up, or are you on your way out now?"

Blinking, Jake scanned the empty room and then glanced at the names in the text. He swung his bag onto his desk and pulled out his laptop. "I have a few more things to check. I'll close up shop on my way out."

The officer waved and left the door open.

Jake fired up his laptop again, his fingers tingling, eager to attack the keyboard. Should he look up the name in the criminal database or just in a search engine? Could this be the first big break in their case?

He started with a search engine and typed in the names. Texts and links spewed over the screen, and he clicked on the first one.

The article headline said it all, and he read it aloud to the empty room. "'Buck Harmon, Foster Father, Brutally Killed by Foster Child.'"

As soon as he read that the foster child who had murdered Buck was a sixteen-year-old female whose name was not being released because she was a juvenile, he didn't have to read any more. He knew her identity.

It was Marilyn Monroe Lake. Kyra Chase was a killer.

Chapter Ten

After the emotional meeting with Andrea's parents, Kyra stepped into the hushed atmosphere of the Santa Monica Public Library and inhaled the scent of musty pages that permeated the air despite the electronic age of digital everything. The public libraries had always been her refuge, and that comforting smell still brought her peace even though her mission today filled her with anxiety.

Brandon Nguyen was able to trace the IP address behind the email from "La Prey," as she'd decided to call him, and that IP address led to this library.

The fact that this was her local library, the one closest to her apartment, filled her with a kind of shivery dread.

Someone who knew about her past had been in this library sending an email to her work address, taunting her, threatening her, trying to frighten her. She didn't know what she hoped to find here. The phantom emailer was long gone. The librarian was not going to hand over any library records or CCTV video to her.

However, the librarian might hand it over to the police, specifically a homicide detective investigating a serial killer.

Kyra wandered to the row of computers where the silence had been invaded by clicking keys and the soft giggles of high school students pretending to do homework. She trailed her hand across the keyboards of three unoccupied computers.

An old homeless woman on the last computer in the row looked up. "Psst."

Kyra raised her eyebrows and met a pair of lively dark eyes set in a leathery face besieged by lines running every which way. "Me?"

"Yeah, you." The woman drew herself up in the chair, pinning her sagging shoulders to the back. "You need to see the reference librarian to use the computers."

"Thanks for the tip." Kyra's gaze darted to the monitor in front of the woman, ablaze with pictures of gaunt models displaying haute couture, then dropped to the baggy gray Santa Monica College sweatshirt covering the woman's form like a sack and what looked like men's black slacks folded up at the ankle to reveal a dirty pair of sneakers with a hole in the toe.

Kyra's nose stung. "C-can I pay you for that advice?"

The woman's eyes lit up. "Well, that's what I'm here for. I'm the information desk…when I'm not designing clothes."

Two girls at the high school study table behind the

computers sniggered and snorted. Kyra whipped her head around and gave the girls a hard stare.

The grins died on their lip-glossed mouths, and they hunched over their laptops.

Kyra reached into her purse and pulled a twenty out of her wallet. She slid it beneath the woman's keyboard. "Will that be enough?"

The homeless woman snatched it, and the bill disappeared among the folds of her clothes. "That will do."

"Do you come here every day and, um…work?"

The woman nodded.

"I suppose there are a lot of people using these computers over the course of a day."

"All the famous designers work here." The woman brushed a hand down the front of her sweatshirt, and Kyra knew she wasn't going to get anything coherent out of her.

"Everything okay?" A librarian, twirling a pair of glasses between her fingers, glanced between Kyra and the homeless lady.

"I think she wants to check out a computer, Inez." The woman turned back to her own screen, dismissing both of them.

"Thanks, Yolanda." The librarian, Inez, smiled at Kyra. "Is that right?"

"No, but I do want to talk to you about the computers."

Inez gestured with her glasses. "Follow me."

The librarian scooted behind the reference counter and faced Kyra across the smooth surface littered with flyers and cards. Inez had put her glasses back on, making her look more formidable.

Kyra put on her best therapist's smile—soothing, nonthreatening, understanding.

"I have a—" Kyra glanced over her shoulder and hunched toward Inez "—bit of a stalking problem."

"Oh, no." Inez pressed three fingers against her rather pale lips.

"Someone has been sending me unwanted emails from a bogus email address. I had a friend of mine who's in IT track down the IP address of the sender, and it came back to one of your computers here in the library." Kyra swept her arm behind her as if to indict the entire library in this stalker's crime.

"That's terrible." Inez's fingers trailed from her lips to her throat, and if she had pearls, she'd be clutching them. "You don't think Yolanda is responsible, do you?"

"Oh, no, no. I sort of have an idea who it is, and I'd like to catch him in the act. You know, have some proof to wave in his face." Kyra folded her hands on the counter on top of a stack of flyers announcing a story time.

"That's terrible. I had a stalker once." Inez slid her glasses to the tip of her nose and whispered, "My ex-husband."

Pursing her lips, Kyra shook her head. "Even when you know who it is, it can be frightening. Sometimes *because* you know who it is, it's even more frightening."

"I agree." Inez readjusted her glasses, which magnified her eyes. She waited quietly.

This was where being a cop came in handy. Kyra said, "I know this is an unusual request, but is there any way you can look at your records and let me know who was at a computer on a particular day at a particular time? Video footage would be even better."

Inez blinked. "I'm sorry. I can't do that."

"All I need is a peek." Kyra crossed her finger over her heart. "I swear, I won't tell anyone. I'm at my wit's end."

"I understand, but it's against our policy. Perhaps if you filed a report with the police. I could release that information to an officer."

"That's the thing." Kyra pressed her palms together and rested her fingers against her chin, silently apologizing to every cop she knew—even Jake. "I think my stalker *is* a cop, which makes things tricky."

"It certainly does. Santa Monica PD?"

Kyra nodded vigorously, hoping she'd never need the assistance of anyone at the SMPD.

"I'm sorry. I just can't." The eyes behind the glasses brightened. "Maybe you could do a stakeout. If he's coming at the same time every day, you could sleuth among the stacks and surprise him."

Kyra stifled a chuckle by smacking her hand over her mouth. When she'd arranged her features into a more fitting expression, she peeled her hand away from her mouth and said, "I might just do that, Inez. Thanks for your time, anyway."

Inez called after her back. "I'll keep my eyes open."

Several library patrons shushed the librarian, and Kyra waved a hand in the air. When she landed outside, she huffed out a breath. She'd known it was a long shot.

If she'd had Jake by her side, getting that information would've been a piece of cake. She could've had him by her side if she'd come clean about her past. She could have shown him the picture of the Harmons and told him why it was a threat to her, and in the very act of telling him, she'd remove the threat.

She'd kept that dark period of her past a secret from everyone, especially guys she was dating. While not wanting to scare anyone off, she'd been scaring men off for years with her secretive nature.

She didn't want to scare off this one.

Striding to her car, she snatched her phone from her purse and called Quinn. "I'm out and about. Do you want me to pick up some food and head over?"

"I was just going to heat up meat loaf. I'll do enough for two." He paused. "Are you all right?"

"Why do you ask?"

"Something in your voice, Mimi."

"I'll be right over."

She drove the short distance from Santa Monica to Venice down traffic-heavy Lincoln. Turning onto the street that led to the canals dropped her into a different world. Most likely Quinn wouldn't have been able to afford a house on the canals, blocks from Venice Beach, on his detective's salary, but his wife,

Charlotte, had been a bestselling author of thrillers and mysteries and had sunk most of her money into their beach cottage, creating an oasis for Quinn away from the grit and grime of his job.

Jake had the same type of getaway with his home in the Hollywood Hills. His creative endeavors on two screenplays had allowed him to buy his own refuge from the job.

Kyra crossed the wooden bridge over the canal and knocked on Quinn's red door. Just as she was about to use her key, he answered.

Stepping over the threshold, she sniffed the air. "Smells yummy in here. Is this meat loaf another contribution from Rose?"

"It is. She's a damned good cook."

"Yeah, she's got something cooking for you, all right." Kyra opened her mouth and winked one eye in an exaggerated fashion.

Quinn poked her in the back. "Go on. At least one of my acquaintances has some home-cooking skills."

"Hey, I'm very good at picking up the phone and ordering." She breezed past Quinn into the kitchen. "You have any beers?"

"Now you're encouraging me to drink? You're usually trying to hide them from me." He sat on a stool at the counter that separated the kitchen from the living room. "Bad day?"

She popped her head out of the fridge, clutching two cold ones in her hands. "Bad, scary, frustrating."

His bushy brows rose to his gray hair. "Scary? You're okay?"

"I'm fine." She twisted the caps from the bottles and shoved a beer across the counter to Quinn's hands, gnarled by arthritis but still able to grip a gun. "I suppose I should start at the beginning."

Taking a sip of beer, he squinted at her through one eye. "I know the beginning, Kyra."

"Sometime after that—" she chugged down some of her drink and wiped the back of her hand across the suds on her lips "—Matt Dugan decided it was a good idea to leave me his worldly possessions."

"That Harley? I'd take that off your hands if I could ride it."

"That bike's getting a new home. Anyway, Matt's parole officer told Jake about my inheritance, and Jake asked if he could come with me to Matt's apartment. He thinks Matt might have been in touch with Jordy, the first copycat killer, because of the playing cards he was leaving me."

"Is Jake wrong?" Quinn folded his hands around the damp bottle.

"I'm not sure." She then told Quinn about the search of Matt's room and the picture of the Harmons she'd taken from his dresser. "Jake saw the picture before I snatched it, but I'm not sure he made any connection to me."

"You're keeping things from him again." Quinn dragged his fingernail through the foil label on the bottle.

"It got worse." She drank more beer for confidence and relayed the rest of the story about the key to Matt's storage container and how she'd set the whole thing on fire to keep Jake from seeing the newspaper clippings and pictures of her Matt had saved.

Quinn set the bottle down on the ceramic tile so hard she thought he'd cracked it. "Kyra, you could've killed yourself and Jake. What the hell were you thinking?"

"I didn't think the whole place would turn into a fireball."

"Did Jake suspect you?"

"I don't know." She lifted and dropped her shoulders. Would he have attempted to make love to her if he thought she'd knowingly torched a storage container with both of them in it? She tapped her finger along her buzzing bottom lip. Maybe.

"Now you want to tell him what you did."

She held up her hand. "Wait. It gets worse. I haven't even told you about the email yet."

"You'd better slow down." He jabbed a crooked finger at her half-empty beer bottle cradled possessively between her hands. "Or you won't be coherent enough to tell me anything."

"When I was at the station, someone sent me an email and attached that same picture of the Harmons."

"Can't blame Matt for that one. The man's dead." Quinn scratched his grizzled chin.

"I realize that, thanks. I did ask our IT guy to trace the IP address, and it came back to the library in Santa Monica. Obviously, it's someone who wants to hide his identity."

"It could be the same person who hired Matt to harass you. Now that Matt's gone, this person has to do his own dirty work."

"I'm pretty sure that's the case. I haven't told you the rest of the storage unit story."

"There's more? It's not enough you set it on fire. Did you blow it up, too?"

"No, but Jake rescued one of the boxes from the unit that didn't burn. I didn't care if he had that box because I'd already checked it out, and as far as I could tell, it contained a bunch of scrap paper and receipts." She took a tiny sip of beer, watching Quinn over the bottle.

"Let me guess. It has more pictures in it."

"Wrong, but when Jake and I were going through the box at my place…"

She stopped when Quinn quirked his eyebrows up and down. "You invited Jake to your apartment?"

"He just showed up with the box." She flicked her fingers in the air. "As I was saying, when we were going through the box, I saw a scrap of paper with the same name as the one in the email address."

She didn't intend to tell Quinn she'd seen that piece of paper while in the throes of passion in Jake's arms. Quinn was a father figure to her, and you just didn't tell your dad stuff like that—even though he would've approved wholeheartedly.

"There's your connection. Unusual name?" Quinn cocked his head.

"Yeah—La Prey. That was in the email address

with the picture attachment, and that name was printed on a piece of paper in Matt's storage unit."

"La Prey? What does that mean?" Quinn slid from the stool. "I'd better get the meat loaf out of the oven."

"I have no idea. It could also be LA Prey, like Los Angeles prey, like I'm his prey." She grabbed plates from the cupboard, feeling lighter already. It always helped to confess her sins to Quinn. He never judged her.

"Mashed potatoes are in the microwave. I didn't want to overheat those."

They suspended discussion of Kyra's crimes and misdemeanors while they bustled around the kitchen, grabbing dishes and food to lay out on the kitchen table by the sliding doors.

When the table was set, Quinn pulled out her chair for her.

She smiled her thanks and said, "Ever since Jake came over here, set the table for dinner and even put a vase of flowers in the center, eating on the couch in front of the TV isn't good enough for you."

"It was nice." He patted her hand as he sat down. "This is nice. Why waste that view off the patio."

She glanced through the glass doors at the moonlit water as it lapped against the rocks that formed the borders for the canals. "You're right. It's beautiful. Charlotte loved this house."

"And you. Charlotte loved you." Quinn's blue eyes watered. "You should've been ours. If I hadn't had that drinking problem, DCFS would've given you to us."

"It was more than that and you know it, Quinn."

"They thought we were too old." He made a spitting noise with his tongue. "Nonsense."

"It wasn't just that, either. Looking back now in my position as a therapist, the social workers probably didn't think it was a good idea for a homicide detective and his wife to adopt a girl he'd rescued from the bloody scene of her mother's murder."

"Why not?" Quinn pounded the handle of his fork on the table. "Who better? I knew what you'd been through. I was in the best position to protect you."

"And you did anyway." She dug into her meat loaf and smacked her lips. "You're right. Rose is a hell of a cook."

Quinn knew she'd never allow him to blame himself for her time in the foster care system. He and Charlotte did everything they could to help and protect her.

With the subject thoroughly changed, Quinn returned to their previous one. "I take it you already went to the library to nose around, and they wouldn't tell you anything."

"Exactly." She scooped up a mound of potatoes and studied it on her fork, wondering how Rose got the potatoes so fluffy.

"I know who could've helped with that if you'd told him." Quinn swirled the last sip of beer in his bottle and then downed it, daring her to disagree with him.

She couldn't. "Believe me, I wished more than once for Jake at my side."

Quinn shoved his plate away and pointed at the kitchen counter next to the landline phone he still had plugged into the wall. "Hand me a piece of paper and the pen by the phone."

Kyra hopped up from her chair, taking their plates with her. After she'd placed them in the sink, she retrieved a memo pad and pen from the counter. She smacked them down in front of Quinn and took her seat, scooting it closer to his.

He tested the pen with a blue scribble in the upper-right corner of the pad of paper. "Okay, Matt planted playing cards for you during the first copycat killer spree. He hinted to Jake that someone had paid him to do it. Matt dies of a drug overdose before spilling the beans."

Despite the way Quinn clutched the pen, his writing was neat and sure as he marked down each point.

"Then Matt leaves you everything he has, including pictures from your foster care with the Harmons. You destroy one of those pictures and someone named La Prey sends you the same pic as an attachment to an email." He glanced up, his blue eyes clear and bright. "How am I doing?"

She gave him a thumbs-up. "So far, so good."

"You then discover a piece of paper with that same unusual name among Matt's things, indicating a connection between Matt, the playing cards, the email and the pictures."

She planted her elbows on the table and said,

"I didn't want to believe it, but it sounds like this La Prey person did pay Matt to plant the cards and maybe intended to use him for other…pranks. When Matt died, La Prey picked up the mantle and carried on by himself. But why? And what does any of this have to do with the copycat killers?"

"We need to find La Prey." Quinn shook a finger at her. "You need to tell Jake everything—yes, even why you got rid of that picture of the Harmons. He can help you. I have a good feeling about that guy, and not just because he's an LAPD homicide detective."

"What if he…?" Kyra sawed her bottom lip, the memory of Jake's kisses tingling.

Quinn smacked the table between them. "Stop right there. If he can't understand why you did what you did, he's not the man I thought he was, and he's not worthy of you. Your deception is a different matter."

"What does that mean?"

"I mean, young lady, when you constantly lie to people, you erode their trust in you. Jake may be able to forgive you for your actions—he might have a harder time forgiving your deception."

Quinn's words pained her heart, and she tapped her chest. "It's even worse. His wife cheated on him with a coworker."

"Then you face the consequences, but you tell him the truth—if not for your relationship with him, then for the case. You're withholding important information."

"I know you're right." She stabbed a finger at his list of events. "Put down 'Kyra comes clean' in your bullet points there."

He waved the memo pad in the air. "I'm not done yet. I'm interested in this name, La Prey. Is that how Matt wrote it down, as two words with a space between them?"

"No, I just say it that way for convenience. Matt and the email address had it all run together as one word—*laprey*. Here, I'll show you." She took the notepad from his hand and picked up the pen. She carefully printed out the name and turned the pad toward Quinn.

He studied the pad for several seconds and then held out his hand for the pen. Clutching the pen, he hunched over the paper, poking at each letter. Then he wrote something beneath it and looked up at Kyra, the lines on his face etched even deeper than usual.

She caught her breath. "What's wrong?"

"*Laprey* is an anagram. It's not only advisable that you tell Jake what's going on—it's imperative."

He shoved the paper toward her, and with her heart galloping in her chest, she read the rearranged letters—*player*.

Chapter Eleven

Jake pushed the computer from his lap, putting distance between himself and the seamy story of a foster parent abusing his charges and the one foster kid in his charge who fought back—stabbing Buck Harmon to death.

He had no doubt the unnamed teen was Kyra Chase.

He rubbed his eyes and then trained them on the view from his window, a sheet of glass that took up the whole wall, bringing the glittering lights of the city into his home. You'd think he'd want to get away from the city, with its evil and darkness, but from up here it looked…enchanted. When he was in this house, looking down at the lights, he could remember all the good, all the decent people.

His gaze wandered to his open laptop, and his blood pounded in his temples as he studied the smug face of Buck Harmon. He knew some foster parents did it for the money; he also knew so many more who did it from the goodness of their hearts. He saw those people when he looked down from his perch in the Hollywood Hills.

The headlights of a car moved across the window as it pulled into his driveway. He pushed up from the couch and peered outside at Kyra's compact stopping behind his car.

The knots in his gut that had been unraveling tightened. Why was she here? What was he going to say to her? If he admitted he knew about her past, she'd accuse him of snooping. If he pretended he knew nothing, she'd sense something was off. Billy was right—Kyra knew people. She'd gone into the right field.

Before he had time to decide how to play it, his doorbell rang. He practically dragged his feet to answer it, when normally he'd be jumping out of his skin at a visit from Kyra.

He swung open the door, and he didn't even get a chance to say hello. She charged past him, her blond hair loose and messy, her eyes glassy and bright.

She took several steps into the room and then spun around, throwing her hands in front of her as if offering him something that wasn't there.

"I have something to tell you—several things to tell you."

He nodded, his jaw seemingly locked in place.

"That picture you saw in Matt's mirror, the one of the family? That was our foster family, the one Matt and I shared. The parents were Buck and Lori Harmon, and I killed Buck Harmon when I was sixteen. Stabbed him."

She seemed to run out of steam, and he gaped at her like an idiot. She took his silence as encouragement, and she wound herself up again, throwing back her shoulders and pacing to the window.

"I'm not proud of what I did, but he deserved it. When I was living with the Harmons, I discovered that Buck was molesting the younger girls. I tried to tell my caseworker at DCFS, but she didn't believe me, and the girls all denied it—because they were scared. Even Quinn couldn't help. The social worker wouldn't even move me out of the home, not that I really wanted to leave the younger girls. The Harmons were the only ones willing to take…troubled teens.

"I tried to protect the girls. I—I told Buck he could have me instead if he left them alone. Do you know what he said?" She twisted her head over her shoulder to meet his eyes.

Jake's stomach turned, but he said quietly, "No."

"He told me I was too old." She snorted, which turned into a sob. "He liked them young and fresh, wasn't interested after they hit puberty."

Jake's hands curled into fists, and he felt like smashing them through the plate-glass window. "You took out the trash."

She turned toward him and flattened her hands against the window, her blue eyes wide, the lights of the city still reflected in their depths. "It was self-defense. One night when he came for one of the girls, I was there to stop him. He smacked me across the face and brandished a knife. Told me he'd kill Sophie if I didn't watch him defile her and take pictures for him, and then he'd kill me."

Although Jake wanted to reach for her, he knew better. He stuffed his hands in the pockets of his jeans and froze in the middle of the room. The news stories had confirmed the killing was in self-defense without going into this level of rancid detail.

"Something snapped inside me." She formed a cross over her chest with both hands. "When he held the knife to Sophie's throat, I went for him. Used a few tricks I'd learned from Quinn and was able to disarm him. Didn't hurt that Buck was on his third six-pack. I got the knife from him, but he didn't stop. He laughed. Then he punched me in the stomach and lunged for Sophie. I lunged for him."

Her voice hitched at the end, and he couldn't hold back any longer. He launched toward her and wrapped his arms around her stiff body. A tremble rolled through her frame, and he stroked his hand down her back.

She spoke into his shoulder, her voice muffled. "There was so much blood. Sophie screamed and woke up the entire household. Buck's wife, Lori, knew about the abuse, and she didn't do anything to stop it. She didn't do anything to help Buck at the end, either."

"She called the police?"

"I did." She broke from his embrace and stepped back, her eyes searching his face. "Lori didn't make a move to do anything. The younger kids were hysterical. Matt wasn't home. I was in shock, but I knew what I had to do."

"Did the police arrest you?"

She ran a hand through her tangled hair. "They took me into custody and they read me my rights, but they didn't handcuff me. I told them to call Quinn and Charlotte. They were with me when the cops questioned me."

"That must've been…traumatic." She'd wandered away from him, not needing or wanting his comfort. He licked his lips. "I—I understand why you wouldn't want to tell people about what happened, but I'm glad you told me."

She'd stopped at the edge of the couch, and her back straightened as if a rod had replaced her spine. Cranking her head toward him, she said, "Looks like I didn't have to tell you. You already discovered everything on your own."

His heart stopped for a second and resumed pounding at a furious pace, the blood pulsing against his ears. His gaze shifted past her to the open laptop on the couch, Buck Harmon smirking at him from the screen.

He lowered his voice. "I did find out about the Harmons."

Holding his breath, he watched the emotions arch across her face and braced for an explosion.

Kyra's shoulders sagged and she dropped to the arm of the couch, her feet spread apart and her knees pinned together, looking like a chastised schoolgirl. Not what he expected from her.

He kept his breath pent up, his muscles rigid—just in case.

"I don't blame you." She raised her eyes to his face, her cheeks pale. "Your instincts were right."

He released a long breath through his teeth, which came out as a whistle. "What do you mean?"

"I had a beer at Quinn's, and I could use another."

He sprang into action, heading for the kitchen. He grabbed two beers from the fridge and pointed one at the couch. "Sit down. Glass?"

"Glass? I'm ready to mainline it."

A grin cracked his stiff face, and he twisted off the caps. He joined her on the couch, shutting his laptop with a snap on Harmon's smug face and putting it on the coffee table.

"I'm all ears."

"You've been all ears since I got here. Feel free to jump in at any time." She cleared her throat, swigged some beer and told him about the email she'd received at work with the Harmon family picture as an attachment.

"It obviously didn't come from Matt Dugan." Jake snapped his fingers. "Is that why you were in deep discussion with Brandon Nguyen? You were trying to find out where the email came from?"

"The Santa Monica Public Library, but I'll get to that in a minute." She dropped her lashes. "First, I need to tell you why I, uh, went cold last night in the middle of…everything."

Jake choked on his beer and it foamed from his nostrils. When Kyra opened up, she really went all out. "I thought you just weren't feeling it with me."

"Yeah, right." Color washed into her cheeks and

she took another sip of beer. "It's because I saw a piece of paper among Matt's things with the same name as that email."

"La Prey?" Jake furrowed his brow. The name that made no sense. "You didn't tell me about it because you'd have to have told me about the email and the picture."

She laced her fingers around the bottle. "Yeah. Sorry."

She didn't have to apologize for wanting to keep that bit of her past hidden. How much trauma could one girl take?

He coughed. "You have the email, the picture and the connection to Matt. Did you have any luck at the library?"

"What do you think?"

"I think the librarian told you to pound sand."

"Exactly."

"I can help you with that."

"Exactly."

"This laprey probably did pay Matt to plant the cards during the killing spree of the copycat, and now he's taunting you with that picture of the Harmons during this second wave of copycat murders. He could be connected to the killers, Kyra."

"There's more, Jake. Even with all that info, I was telling myself that Matt's involvement and even La Prey's involvement had nothing to do with the serial killers. I was still planning to keep all of this from you…until tonight."

"What happened tonight?" He hunched forward

slightly, watching her lips, not wanting to miss one word that fell from them. Quinn must've convinced her to come clean.

"I was going through everything with Quinn, and he started writing out the events on a piece of paper. When it came to La Prey, he wrote it out as it appeared on the email address and Matt's scribbling. Here, I'll show you." She ripped off a piece of paper from a notebook on his desk and grabbed a pen. She printed out the letters on the paper and shoved it in front of him on the table.

He looked at the word for just a second. She didn't have to tell him why she was here tonight confessing everything. His gaze flew to her face. "La Prey is an anagram for *player*."

It HAD TAKEN Jake less time than Quinn to see what was right in front of their faces. She'd been the only one to miss it. Had Matt missed it? Matt had a lot of issues, but he was no killer. He wouldn't help one, either.

Kyra crumpled the paper in her fist. "I was so fixated on the LA part, I couldn't see past it. I mean, it can't *be* him…can it? It's just someone using the name to terrorize me for some reason."

Jake tapped one finger on his knee, his hazel eyes dark and flat. "Who else knows your identity besides me, Quinn and Matt?"

"I don't know." She pressed a hand against her midsection to still the butterflies that kicked up every time she thought about this. "There were people at the time who knew, of course. The cops, the social workers. If you noticed, the news stories about Buck's...death didn't mention that the foster child who did the dirty work was the daughter of a homicide victim. That would've been a juicy story, but the press didn't run with it. Still, I'm guessing some of the cops knew. That's why they were so sympathetic."

"Captain Castillo?"

She blinked at him. "He was around, so maybe. I wasn't taken to your division. It was LAPD jurisdiction, but it was a different station. Why Castillo?"

"Not sure." He picked at the soggy label on his bottle. "I suppose it wouldn't be too difficult for someone involved—social worker, cop, medical worker—to have kept tabs on you through the years and followed your name change. If someone wasn't watching you, Marilyn Monroe Lake could morph into Kyra Leigh Chase without a hitch, but if someone had his or her eye on you, was checking up on you periodically, that name change may not have been so seamless."

The creepiness of someone watching her that closely receded slightly with the realization that he knew her middle name. "We're back to cops again. Why? Why would someone be tracking me like that?"

"Matt Dugan did."

"Matt was obsessed with me."

"What was Matt's response to Buck's death?"

Her cheeks grew warm and she pressed the cool,

damp bottle against her face. "He thought it was the raddest thing ever. Kept making excuses as to why he'd never done it himself. Started looking at me a little differently after that."

"Do you think it led to his obsession?"

"Absolutely. He fancied us a modern-day Bonnie and Clyde going on some crime spree together. Quinn had different ideas. That's when he and Charlotte finally got me for good. DCFS was just happy to get rid of me at that point." She clasped her hands between her knees. "But that's Matt, and Matt's dead. Who else would want to keep tabs on me?"

Jake traced a pattern on the thigh of his jeans with the tip of his finger. Without looking up, he said, "When I confronted you about the playing cards during the first copycat killings, you mentioned that The Player was still out there. Do you still believe that?"

"Well, he is, isn't he? Quinn never caught him. He stopped his killing spree. Nobody ever confessed, no witnesses ever came forward. He must be out there somewhere." Her gaze shifted to the huge window that took up one wall of Jake's living room.

He had no drapes or blinds on the window, but he didn't need them. He was high enough on the hill that nobody could see inside his place. He could see them, but they couldn't see him—sort of a metaphor for his job.

Jake said, "He could be dead."

"Could be. Hope so. But if he is—" Kyra twisted

her fingers in her lap "—who's this Player torment-ing me?"

"If he isn't, why would he be taunting you now?"

Her stomach flip-flopped. She'd never talked about any of this stuff with anyone other than Quinn. The conversation with Jake stripped her bare—and not in a good way.

Crossing her arms over her chest, she asked, "What do you mean?"

"Stay with me for a minute." He held up one fin-ger, a shred of the beer label hanging off his finger-nail. "If The Player isn't dead and he's behind the playing cards and the email, why? Why would he contact you now?"

"Not sure. Maybe because of the renewed inter-est in his crimes due to the copycats."

"Okay, I'll go along with that, but does he even know who you are? Does he know about Matt and the Harmons?"

"Good questions." She picked up her beer again, less eager to down the remaining sips now that it had done its job of taking off the edge while she'd come clean to Jake. "I asked Quinn about that, and he's al-ways been pretty vague. The news reports at the time did mention that Jennifer Lake's daughter had been asleep in the house during her mother's murder and that she had discovered the body. That's all true."

"The accounts I read never mentioned your name, showed your picture or gave any details about your fate. For all anyone knew, you could've left the state with grandparents or other relatives."

Kyra's throat tightened and she gulped down the rest of the beer after all. "Well, that didn't happen."

"The Player wouldn't have known that. He had no way of tracking you, so he wouldn't know who you were now, especially now with the name change. Maybe that's why…" Jake broke off and rubbed his jaw.

"Why what?" The fluttering continued in her belly, almost as if there was something to be discovered around the corner that she didn't want to know.

"I know Quinn and Charlotte never officially adopted you, but you did go to live with them when you…left the Harmons. When you changed your name, why didn't you take Quinn's last name? Kyra Quinn has a nice ring to it."

"I wanted to. I'd planned on it…" She put her hand to her throat and met Jake's eyes. "Quinn didn't want me to. I was hurt, but he and Charlotte made up some excuse, which I accepted at the time, and then proved in a thousand different ways it wasn't because they didn't want me. You think Quinn didn't want me to take his name because he didn't want The Player to know who I was."

"I think so." Jake squeezed her hand, which was lying limply in her lap. "Not that he would be looking for you. Why should he? That's what I'm thinking now. Why would The Player, after getting away with several murders, come out of the woodwork now? Just because some sickos decided to copy his demented crimes?"

"Prison. You know better than I do that serial killers stop when they die or are imprisoned. Maybe he's been in jail all this time."

"Still doesn't explain how he found you. Maybe the person taunting you now is just some messed-up acquaintance of Matt's. Matt got drunk or high, told the guy all about you, and he picked it up and ran with it. I'd sure like to talk to him, see if he had any connection to Jordy Cannon. He might even lead us to Andrea's and Crystal's killer." He reached across her to grab her beer bottle. "I'm glad you told me everything."

She nudged the toe of her sandal against the laptop on the coffee table. "Too late. I didn't have to tell you. You found out on your own from Billy's friend at DCFS."

Jake tripped to a stop on his way to the kitchen with the bottles in one hand. "It didn't happen like that."

His voice had dropped, and she twisted on the couch to face him fully. "You don't have to lie. I saw Tara's name on your phone, and I asked Billy about her later—told him I was jealous."

Jake's eyes widened briefly. "I did talk to Tara, but she didn't give me the goods…couldn't. Your file at DCFS is locked down. Matt's, too, for the same time period."

"Oh." She skimmed a hand through her hair. "I have Quinn to thank for that, too."

"I imagine you do." He continued on his way to the large kitchen and edged around the granite island in the center.

She pushed up from the couch and followed him. As he dropped the bottle in the recycling bin, she sat on the chair at the end of the island and planted her elbows on the granite. "How did you find out about the Harmons and what happened there? Did Matt have some paperwork in that box I missed?"

"No." Jake folded his arms and wedged his lower back against the counter.

A muscle twitched at the corner of her mouth. Jake didn't want to tell her. Who was left to betray her? Quinn never would, not even to Jake.

"It—it's okay, Jake. I won't be upset. Quinn made me see that I should've been telling you everything for the sake of the case."

He pushed away from the counter and reached for a shelf on the other side of the kitchen from her. He yanked his phone from the charger and tapped the display.

He placed the phone in front of her and said, "This is how I knew."

Chapter Twelve

Kyra swallowed when she saw the text message calling out the Harmons. "Who sent this?"

"I don't have a clue. I tried texting back. I tried calling the number. It's like the text was sent and the phone turned off." He spun the phone back toward him with one finger. "Unlike you with the email, I haven't had a chance to put a trace on the phone, but my guess?"

She answered for him. "It's a burner."

"Probably stuffed in a trash bin, as we speak. Doesn't mean I can't try. Remember when we thought Jordy had called from a burner phone, and it turned out he'd stolen one from Rachel Blackburn."

"That definitely helped crack the case. Maybe this guy made the same mistake as Jordy." Kyra folded her hands on the smooth granite as if waiting to be schooled by the great detective. "How did this person know you were looking for my foster family?"

Jake tugged on his earlobe. "That's a question I've been avoiding. Who would know?"

Kyra raised her hand and wiggled her fingers,

ticking off each one with a name. "Tara, the social worker. Billy, if Tara told him. Matt, who's dead. Quinn, probably. Anyone who overheard you at the station."

"Nobody overheard me."

"That's what you think. I saw the display with Tara's name, and I saw your text exchange with Matt last month. People who are hell-bent on discovering information will find a way."

He swept some nonexistent crumbs from the counter into his palm. "None of those names you mentioned makes sense. If Tara had the Harmons' name, she would've given it to me. Billy wouldn't know or care. As you pointed out, Matt's dead. Quinn wouldn't betray you if I offered him The Player on a silver platter."

"Unless—" she sucked in her bottom lip "—Quinn told you to force me to come clean to you about everything. Quinn has been warning me that the stuff happening to me might be connected to the copycat killers."

"Quinn wouldn't send me an anonymous text from a burner phone, though. He's not that kind of guy. He'd tell you he was going to do it, and then he'd call me directly and tell me."

"You're right." She drummed her fingers on the surface of the island. "It must be La Prey—I mean, the other player. He seemed to know that I'd destroyed the picture of the Harmons I took from Matt's apartment. He knew you were looking into my past."

"He could be making some educated guesses. I was going to meet Matt before he died. Maybe player just assumed I was digging into your past." Jake circled a finger in the air. "He's not some omniscient creature."

"Sure feels like it." She rubbed the goose bumps racing up her arms. "And can I ask you a favor?"

"I figure I owe you a few for snooping into your past."

Wrinkling her nose, she waved her hand. "Forget that, but could you not call this new threat against me The Player? Sounds too much like the old threat against me—or at least my mother. I prefer to think of him as La Prey, sounds almost refined."

"Done. I want to track him down, not just to make him stop torturing you, but to find out why he's so interested in The Player and this current killing spree. He might know these guys."

"You're checking out Jordy Lee Cannon's friends and associates, right?"

"Yeah, though the fact that he's dead doesn't make it easy. If I could've kept him alive, taken him into custody, questioned him…" Jake ground his fist into his palm. "I could've made him talk, give up his secrets and his motivation."

She said in a small voice without looking up, "I'm afraid that's my fault. If I hadn't gone after him myself, he never would've taken me hostage and you wouldn't have had to shoot him."

"We caught him faster because of you. If he had gotten away that night, he might've committed another murder. You may have saved someone's life that night, so don't beat yourself up."

Jake's words gave her a warm glow, and she glanced up at him through her lashes. He hadn't had much of a reaction about Buck Harmon, except to say she'd taken out the trash when she had killed him. That seemed like a typical response from a cop.

Bracing her hands against the cool countertop, she started. "I didn't want to tell you about Buck for the same reason I didn't want to tell you I was the daughter of one of The Player's victims. I know it's a past that has formed me, but I don't want it to define who I am today. I can change my identity, but I'll never erase those experiences. I don't necessarily want to erase them. I just don't want to be judged by them, even if that judgment is on my side and takes the form of pity. I don't want people walking around on eggshells in my presence. I'm sorry I lied to you. I'm sorry I hid things from you."

He held up a hand. "It's…understandable."

"When Quinn worked out that anagram, I realized how important it was to tell you everything. Still, it was more than that." She peeled her hand from the counter and ran it along the tail of the tattoo on his left forearm, snaking out of the arm of his T-shirt. "I knew if I ever hoped to have some kind of relationship with you, I'd have to tell you all about my ugly past."

His arm tensed and corded beneath her fingertips. "Do you hope to have some kind of relationship with me?"

His voice, all rough around the edges, sent a thrill

to her core, and she dug her fingertips into his flesh. "I do, if I haven't scared you off."

Keeping his arm in her grip, he hunched forward across the island and wedged a finger beneath her chin. "Do I look like the kind of man who scares easily?"

Her lashes fluttered as she took in the strong jaw, set in determination, and the spark in his hazel eyes. She breathed out one word. "No."

Her breath hitched in her throat as he circled the island and planted himself in front of her. He ran one hand through her hair and leaned in for a kiss, slanting his mouth across hers; his lips, slightly chapped, caressed hers, demanding more from her.

For the first time in a long time, she was willing to give more. She'd told Jake more about herself than she'd ever admitted to another man. It was a step, a first step.

She curled her arms around his neck and hopped from the high chair, hanging against him for a few seconds, her toes brushing the wood floor.

His hand slipped from the back of her head and cupped her face as he rained soft kisses on her lips. She sighed against his mouth, her knuckles brushing his prickly jaw.

He fitted his body with hers along every line, so that his erection pressed against her pelvis. She swayed her hips in a sinuous dance to get him even closer.

His breath hot on her cheek, he grabbed her hand and pulled her away from the kitchen. She tripped as he veered course from the stairs that must lead to his bedroom in favor of the living room with its sprawling view of the city. Before she had a second to wonder where he was taking her, his cell phone rang.

She'd never heard that particular ringtone from his phone before. It must've been coming from his private cell—he wouldn't have a song from a boy band on his work phone.

The sound of the ringtone stopped Jake dead in his tracks. He put a finger to her thrumming lips. "I'm so sorry. I have to answer this."

She nodded and almost collapsed on her jelly legs when he released her and returned to the kitchen. He picked up the phone that had been charging next to his work phone.

With his back to her, he answered. "Fiona, what are you doing up so late? Isn't it a school day tomorrow?"

Fiona? Kyra's lips lifted on one side. His daughter.

As Jake launched into a conversation that could only be with an adolescent, Kyra tiptoed to her purse, hitched it over one shoulder and slipped out his front door.

OVER FIONA'S WHINING, Jake heard the soft click of his front door. He twisted his head around, taking in the empty living room and the vacant spot where Kyra had dropped her purse earlier.

He muttered, "Damn."

Fiona interrupted the tirade against her mother

and her tyrannical rule, and said, "Dad, you're not supposed to curse in front of me."

"I'm sorry, Fiona. You're right." He sat heavily on the chair Kyra had occupied earlier, her scent, like rosebushes through an open window, still wafting in the air. "You need to listen to your mother and…"

"Brock. My stepfather's name is Brock, Dad."

"I know that." He gave a secret smile into the phone. "When you're with them—"

"Which is most of the time."

His daughter's barbed words pricked him. When had she gotten so…grown-up? "It is, so it's important that you follow their rules."

"Christmas. You said I could come for Christmas break." She heaved a sigh that gushed over the line. "I am not going to Japan with Mom and Brock. I don't want to go to Japan."

"Your mother and I still need to discuss that." Meaning he'd ask and Tess would say no.

"Were you busy when I called? Watcha working on?"

His work was not fit to discuss with a fourteen-year-old girl, even one with a fascination for true crime. Where the hell had she gotten that and why had Tess allowed it? He knew something had gone amiss when Fiona had visited him last year and asked him to take her to Cielo Drive, where the Manson Family had committed their most famous crime.

Who was he kidding? Tess hadn't allowed that. She'd been horrified when Jake told her about Fiona's request, and promptly blamed him.

"I'm working on a case, just like I always am, but I was watching TV when you called and thinking about bed." Well, that last part wasn't too far off the mark. He *had* been thinking about going to bed… with Kyra.

"Boring." Fiona made a disgusted sound. "Just let Mom know I'm for sure coming to your place for Christmas."

"We will continue to discuss it, I promise. Remember, fighting with your mother over everything is not going to help your case."

"All right. Love you, Daddy."

Jake's throat got tight just like it did every time he heard those words from Fiona. God knew what he'd done to deserve them. "Love you, too, Fiona."

When the call ended, he put his phone back on the charger and texted Kyra to let him know when she got home. He didn't know what game was being played, but this guy knew too much about Kyra's past to be ignored.

And before these pranks turned physical, Jake intended to put a stop to them.

THE FOLLOWING MORNING, Jake rolled out of bed with heavy eyes and a fog invading his brain. His single beer the night before hadn't resulted in a hangover. He'd call it a Kyra Chase hangover.

He stepped into the shower and cranked on the water. Two nights in a row, he'd had his plans for seduction waylaid—once at her place, once at his. Maybe next time, they should try for neutral ground.

He scrubbed away most of the residue of disappointment from his body with soap and warm water and got ready for work.

As he drove to the station, he had one thought on his mind…two thoughts—tracking down the phone that had left him the text message about the Harmons, and Kyra.

When he got to the task force conference room at the station, his gaze slid to the side, taking in Kyra's empty desk. She'd texted him when she made it back to her place, not including anything else in her message—no apology, no explanation as to why she bolted.

Kyra must've known it was his daughter on the line. The kid scared her away. She knew he had a daughter, but maybe it was another matter to hear him actually speaking to her. Kyra didn't strike him as the motherly sort, so she just might back away from any relationship that included children.

He shook his head and grabbed the coffee cup that magically appeared on his desk. Nodding thanks to his partner, he said, "Any luck with the footage in the surrounding areas of the crime scenes?"

"We're getting there." Billy picked up his phone. "I have a few more homeowners to contact."

While Billy made his calls, a pinprick of guilt needled the back of Jake's neck. Billy was hard at work on their case, and he was trying to track down a phone that had texted him about Kyra's foster family.

Jake rolled his shoulders, sloughing off the guilt. He couldn't shake the feeling that Kyra's history was inextricably linked to the killings happening recently. To sort out her past could only help him in this investigation.

He ignored the little voice that hammered in his head telling him that sorting out her past would help him protect her, too.

He got on the phone with the tech guys on the task force and gave them the number that had texted him the info about the Harmons. The techies didn't even ask what connection the text had to the case. They assumed anything the task force leader sent over was valid—and they were right.

As soon as he hung up his desk phone, it rang. "McAllister."

"J-Mac, this is Sergeant Montiel downstairs. We just got a call about a dead body, an apparent homicide, in a home in Los Feliz. Has all the earmarks of your guy."

Through narrowed eyes, Jake scanned the activity in the room—people buzzing around like busy bees. In two seconds, he'd be prodding the beehive.

He took down a few details from Montiel, including the address, and stood up. "We have another body."

His words had an instantaneous effect on the room. People dropped what they were doing. Some rushed from the area. Some picked up phones. Some fired up their computers. Everyone had something to do.

Jake clapped Billy on the back. "Let's hit it, Cool Breeze."

Billy rose from his chair and ducked his head. "Victim?"

"She's not African American, so this freak is an equal-opportunity killer."

Grabbing his jacket, Billy said, "Doesn't make me feel any better."

Jake drove to the crime scene with Billy riding shotgun. Jake shot a sidelong glance at his partner, his jaw tight, his shoulders braced for the crime scene. Jake knew Billy cared just as much about this victim as Andrea and Crystal, but he wouldn't have the added torment of thinking about his sister and her fate. Billy was only cool breeze on the surface. Each murder they investigated burned a hole in Billy's soul. He and his partner dealt with the trauma in different ways, and that trauma never went away.

Jake pulled up to the crime scene, which patrol officers had already marked off. The yellow tape wafted in the light breeze, waving them over in a desultory manner. The neighbors formed knots at various locations along the sidewalk, craning their necks to watch the action. He and Billy would be giving them plenty of action in due time.

They strode up to the officer on the perimeter, his arms folded, his sunglasses repelling anyone who wandered too close. They flashed their badges, and Jake said, "Officers inside?"

The patrolman held up two fingers.

When they reached the second officer, stationed at the front door, Billy said, "Are we the first detectives here?"

Officer Nance stepped aside from the front door, which was gaping open. "When my partner and I saw the vic, we didn't waste time with anyone else. We called Sarge immediately to report to the task force."

"Appreciate it, Nance." Billy held out his fist for a bump and Nance complied, reddening to the roots of his ginger hair.

When Jake stepped into the house, the odor of death tickled his nostrils. The air-conditioning emitted a low hum, but the AC wasn't blasting enough to chill a body.

Jake did a half turn. "Any signs of forced entry, Nance?"

"None, sir."

The officer didn't have to tell them the victim was in the bedroom, most likely in her bed. Jake followed Billy down the short hallway where another two officers stood at the entrance to a room.

"We'll take it from here, boys." Billy jerked his thumb over his shoulder. "If you haven't done so already, check all the doors and windows for break-ins. We have a bunch of lookie-loos out there. Start canvassing. We're especially interested in security systems. Anyone who has a camera, let them know we want the video."

The officers fled the room, one of them absolutely green around the gills.

Jake had pulled on his gloves as he walked into the room and approached the bed where a young woman lay neatly against her pillows, staring sightlessly at the ceiling with the queen of spades between her lips. A splotch of blood stained the covers where the woman's hand with the finger severed must be.

Just as in the other two slayings, the bedclothes were neat and orderly, but the killer had to have been on the bed, over the victim, in the position to strangle her.

Billy used a gloved finger to lift the woman's hair from her neck to expose the angry purple marks on her neck. "These crime scenes are almost antiseptic, aren't they?"

"He's a careful guy. That's why he lies in wait—no struggle, less hassle."

"I'm going to check the closet in the second bedroom. We haven't even been able to tell where he's been hiding in the house."

"It's another house without a camera, though. That's one of his criteria."

"What about the rest of his selection process?" Billy's gaze flicked over the dead woman. The officers hadn't given them her name yet. "At first we thought he might be targeting young African American women. This victim doesn't qualify."

"She's young, lives alone, no camera. She lives in a house, not an apartment, and is probably careless in some way about the security of her home. The killer does not want to work hard."

"Probably stalked her like the others to learn her habits." Billy pointed to the door. "I'm going to have a look in the other rooms, garage, too."

Jake flicked back the covers and peered at the bloody stub on the woman's hand. Fingering the woman's long brown locks, he murmured, "Did you take her hair again, freak?"

He was no expert on hairstyles, but strands of hair on the left side of the woman's head did appear shorter than the ones on the right. He'd taken his trophy.

Eyeing the neat covers, Jake patted them with his gloved hands. As he brushed one hand off the edge of the bed, something crinkled beneath his fingers. He turned his hand over and brought it close to his face.

His heart skipped a beat. Stuck to his glove was a piece of tape. At Andrea's house, he'd felt something sticky on the bedspread, and the lab had identified it as the substance on the back of tape. Now he'd found the tape.

"You left something behind this time, freak." He held up the tape to the light streaming through the bedroom window and sucked in a sharp breath.

"Are you ready for us, J-Mac?" Clive Stewart, their fingerprint tech, hovered at the bedroom door with his black case.

Jake looked up with a smile stretching his lips. "You're just in time, Clive. We have a fingerprint."

Chapter Thirteen

Kyra jerked her head up, nostrils flaring. The mood of the task force room had shifted, and a whispered undercurrent swept through the space, almost ruffling papers in its wake. She held her breath until it reached her corner.

She leaned across her desk and whispered to one of the patrol officers tasked with checking home security video. "What happened?"

He raised his eyebrows, his glance shifting from side to side as if the entire room didn't already know. "Copycat 2.0 just messed up. He left a fingerprint."

Kyra wriggled in her seat like a birthday girl at her own party. "That's fantastic news. I hope he's in the system."

For the next hour, she glanced up every time someone walked into the conference room. Finally Jake came striding in with a kick to his step.

She raised her hand, tentatively, not sure if he was mad at her for skipping out on their…encounter last night.

When he nodded at her and winked, she let out a

long breath and got back to entering family members for Copycat 2.0's latest victim, Mindy Behr. The task force usually let the press dub the serial killers, and 2.0 had taken off after the murder of Crystal Monroe. She preferred it to the Copycat Player, which had been Jordy Lee Cannon's name and had given her a jolt whenever she heard it.

Despite the noise in the task force headquarters, she got lost in her work, tuning it all out until someone behind her cleared his throat. She twisted her head over her shoulder and knew she'd be looking into Jake's hazel eyes. Her radar seemed to pick up his presence.

She held up a finger, added more data to her file and saved it. "Fingerprint, huh? That's huge."

"Yeah. The guy thought he was pretty clever by using tape to get rid of any hairs or fibers on the bedclothes, but he left a piece of it behind. Clive already lifted it, and we're going to enter it into the database." His lips twisted into a frown, and she couldn't help the little shiver that ran down her back at the thought of those lips on hers.

She blinked. "What's wrong?"

"It's not a perfect print, which might prevent us from getting a clean hit."

"But it's something." She glanced over his head to make sure everyone was too busy to listen. "Are you free for lunch?"

"I am, and I have something to tell you." He rose from his crouch. "Hang on. I have a few more things to do."

"How about I meet you at your car? I...uh, need to hit the restroom anyway."

"I'll be there in ten."

Most of the task force had some idea that she and Jake had more than a working relationship, but she didn't want to highlight that fact. She closed her laptop and stuffed it into her bag. She did make a detour to the ladies' room, but only to check her hair and makeup. If he'd agreed to lunch that easily, he must've already forgiven her for leaving his place last night without a word.

She retouched her lipstick, straightened her skirt and smoothed back her ponytail. Lunch *and* information. She'd hit the jackpot today.

Several minutes later, she waited nonchalantly by his unmarked LAPD sedan, pretending she was looking for something in her purse anytime someone walked by.

Jake put her out of her misery by showing up just a short time after her, his long stride eating up the parking lot between them. He beeped his remote before he reached her, and she slid into the passenger seat.

Scooting behind the wheel, he cocked his head at her. "Big hurry, are we?"

"Is it against the rules or something for us to be... more than coworkers?" She tugged her skirt over her knees.

"Are we?" He started the car and turned down the AC. "Seems to me, forces beyond our control are keeping us apart."

"Yeah, about that." She wrinkled her nose. "I'm sorry I dashed out of there. I knew you were talking to your daughter. I—I remembered her name was Fiona. I didn't want to interrupt or make you feel like you had to rush off the phone with your daughter."

"I get it. The call sort of…spoiled the moment."

She opened her mouth, snapped it shut and started again. "Is everything okay? With your daughter, I mean?"

"She's fine." With his hands resting on the top of the steering wheel, he pointed out the windshield. "Dandelion Café okay with you?"

"Perfect." She kept staring at his profile. That was the first question she'd asked about his daughter. Did he not want to tell her about Fiona? Wasn't that what people did in relationships? Opened up?

He glanced at her and flexed his fingers on the wheel. "Just regular teenage angst—she's fourteen. She and her mother argue about everything these days."

"That's normal at her age." She tapped her temple. "I know these things. I wrote the book on teenage angst."

"Yeah, but you—" He broke off, a flash of red on his neck.

"You're right. I had it worse than most, but to every teenager, his or her situation always feels like the worst. Does she have a best friend?"

"I, uh…" The flush on his skin deepened. "She's mentioned a few friends. I'm not sure if she considers one a best friend. Does that make me a terrible father?"

"Of course not." She patted his thigh. "Even if you knew the name of her best friend, it might change tomorrow."

Staring out the window, Jake sucked in his cheek. "I messed up. We were too young for kids. I hadn't even been a cop for a year, and Tess was still in law school."

"But you managed and, despite teenage turmoil, Fiona is a happy kid? Well-adjusted?"

"She seems to be whenever I see her. She does well in school, has friends, plays on the high school soccer team and takes guitar lessons. No boys—that I know of."

Kyra rolled her eyes. "If you're anything like Quinn was when I brought any boys around to meet him, those guys are in for it."

"I hope I get that opportunity." Jake's hands tightened on the wheel before he cranked it to the right. "Maybe we can get a table before it's too crowded."

They snagged a table on the patio with ease. Although the Dandelion was no cop hangout, the hostess seemed to have a soft spot for Jake. What woman wouldn't? He exuded such a tough-guy attitude, you just knew he'd take care of you in a jam. His hotness quotient didn't hurt, either.

How had she been able to walk out on him twice? First time had been for *her* sake, second for his. Maybe fate wasn't smiling on them, but she'd revealed so much to him already that she didn't want to give up on him. And when had fate ever stopped her before?

They sat in the shade on the patio and ordered iced teas.

As Kyra shook out her napkin onto her lap, she said, "Tell me about the fingerprint."

"At the first crime scene I picked up some sticky substance on the bedspread, which turned out to be the glue on the back of tape. I figured then he was patting down the bedclothes and the area to pick up any threads or fibers—clever. I noticed the same thing at Crystal's. I checked for it again at today's crime scene and found a bit of tape. When I held it up to the light—bingo—I saw a fingerprint. His hands must've been dirty when he touched the tape— maybe before he put on his gloves."

"Good. He slipped up." She planted an elbow on the table and rested her chin in her palm. "If he's been arrested before, his prints will be on file. Heck, if he has a driver's license in California, he should have a thumbprint with them."

"It's not like we can run it through the Department of Motor Vehicles database, and the DMV doesn't take a full set for a license. All we have is one finger. It would have to be the same fingerprint with the DMV." He shook off the negative attitude when the drinks came and sucked down his tea straight with no sugar. "But it's something. More will come. I'm feeling confident about the security systems in the areas of the victims' houses. He didn't just appear in one spot and disappear. He had to have walked or driven. We'll get him."

Kyra stirred two packets of sweetener in her tea. "Sometimes I wonder how cops ever solved crimes without DNA and CCTV."

"It was a lot harder, for sure. Look at all the cold cases we have. Anyone who committed a crime prior to 1986 and left DNA has to be sweating bullets today. That knock on the door is gonna come."

"Except for The Player," Kyra said softly into her swirling tea.

"The bastard never left his DNA." Jake tapped one finger on the table. "Weird, how neither the Copycat Player nor Copycat 2.0 has left his DNA at the scene. There's almost always a sexual component to a serial killer's motivation, and yet no rapes, no semen, no DNA."

"We know why Jordy didn't feel the urge to rape his victims. He took his sexual aggressions out on hookers after the slayings." She flattened the empty packets of sweetener with her thumb. "I wonder how this guy satisfies that urge."

Glancing to his right, Jake hunched forward. "God, I hope nobody is listening to this conversation."

"Ugh, you're right." She picked up the menu and scanned the salads and sandwiches. "Is that what you wanted to tell me?"

Jake peered at her over the top of his own menu. "The fingerprint? No, I wanted to tell you about the phone that sent me the text about the Harmons."

"Yes?" She clutched the laminated menu so hard, its edges bit into her fingers.

"As I suspected, it was a burner phone and it's already out of service." He tapped his menu against hers. "Sorry to disappoint you, but we sort of knew this person wasn't going to call from a cell that could be traced."

"Because he called you—a cop. But when he contacted me via email, he couldn't do so completely anonymously, could he? Maybe he figured I wouldn't have the resources to track him down at the library."

Jake said, "You do now. I requested a subpoena for the library's video footage for the day and approximate time you received that email. We'll get to have a look at who sat at those public computers in the library and sent you the photo."

"That's fantastic." She clapped her hands together and held them under her chin as if in prayer, but this man had already answered her prayers. "D-do you think you'll get the subpoena?"

"It's related to a serial killer case. Are you kidding? The mayor would be willing to give me the key to the entire city if it would help me bring in another killer." He stopped talking when the waitress came back to take their orders.

As she watched the waitress approach another table, Kyra whispered, "Do you know Mayor Wexler?"

"I've met him a few times. He's close with Chief Sterling. The guy loves his power."

Kyra closed her lips around her straw. She could

tell Jake a lot more about Ben Wexler than probably even the chief knew, since Wexler's wife, Monica, was her client. Some secrets she still needed to keep from Jake.

They got through the rest of their lunch without a word about murder, rape or DNA, but when it came time to pay the bill, Kyra slapped her hand on the check. "This is mine if you clue me in when you get the subpoena. I want to be looking at that library video with you."

"I wouldn't have it any other way, and—" he pinched the corner of the bill between two fingers and tugged "—you don't need to pick up lunch to bribe me."

"It's not a bribe. I invited you." She yanked the bill from his fingers and fished her debit card from her wallet.

He drove her back to the station. She stopped outside the building and waved him on. "You go ahead. I'm going to make a call outside."

"Good idea. Thanks for lunch." He marched into the station without a second glance.

She hadn't fooled him with her phone-call excuse, but he hadn't objected, either. He must agree with her that it was best to keep their relationship outside of work private—not that coworkers on the task force didn't have lunch together. She'd just had lunch with Billy yesterday, but rumors were not already swirling around her and Billy.

A young woman with black hair waved at her

across the parking lot and then skipped toward her. "Kyra, right?"

Kyra glanced at the woman's tatted-up arm and blinked at the bright eyes and ready smile. "Rachel? Blackburn, right?"

"That's right. I wasn't sure if you'd remember me."

"Of course I do." Kyra waved her hand up and down the woman's casual slacks and blouse, a pair of black flats on her feet. "I didn't recognize you at first with the…uh, makeover."

The last time she'd seen Rachel, when her phone had been stolen by the Copycat Player to report the location of a body, she'd been sporting multiple piercings, heavy, dark makeup and black combat boots.

"Oh, I still inhabit that other persona, but I just got hired as an LAPD dispatcher. Detective McAllister was true to his word and got me in."

"I'm sure Human Resources was blown away by you and didn't even need McAllister's recommendation." Rachel had impressed both her and Jake with her keen perception and intelligence, so much so that Jake had gotten her hooked up with a job as a dispatcher.

"Thanks, but we both know a recommendation from Detective McAllister is worth a lot." Rachel screwed up her mouth. "With *most* people in the department."

Rachel had already discovered that J-Mac had a reputation with the LAPD and not everyone appreciated his tactics.

"Do you like the job so far?"

"I do. It's great. Hoping to learn all I can, finish my degree and then apply for a sworn position."

"I'm sure you'll make a great cop, Rachel." Kyra pointed to the building. "You going inside?"

The two walked into the station together and split up on the first floor. Jake was already hard at work by the time Kyra made it to her desk. Her sandwich and salad should've made her sleepy, but the discovery of Mindy Behr's body that morning had everyone amped up, and phones rang off the hook and spontaneous discussions broke out across the room. Nobody needed coffee with the energy bouncing off the walls, but gallons of the stuff disappeared anyway.

A few hours into the afternoon, Jake caught her eye across the room and tapped his personal cell phone. Two seconds later her own phone buzzed, and she glanced at the text.

As she read Jake's words, her pulse danced in her throat. The judge had signed off on the subpoena for the video at the Santa Monica Public Library. Jake promised to let her know when he planned to head out there to view it.

She texted him back with a thumbs-up emoji and let him know the library was open until nine o'clock this evening and that she had a client at five.

The rest of the afternoon flew by in a blur. At a few minutes before four o'clock, Kyra packed up her laptop and wedged the case on her chair. She sauntered to the back row of desks where J-Mac and Cool Breeze held court and leaned against Billy's desk.

"Everything go okay at the crime scene today?"

"As okay as that kind of thing can go, and of course we collected the print." Billy slumped in his chair and extended his long legs in front of him. "You know, I think I would've been able to keep it together even if the victim had been an African American female, but this experience has given me new resolve to find my sister."

"Really? Are you going to reopen the case?"

"I don't have the authority to do that, and missing person cases don't fall under robbery-homicide anyway. I do, however, have a line on a PI. I'm going to call him and schedule an appointment. I can't work this job and hold my breath every time we get a call on a young Black female, I need to know. My family needs to know."

"Let me know if I can be of any help, Billy." She dropped a hand to his shoulder and squeezed. "I mean that."

Jake had been trying to ignore their hushed conversation from the desk next to Billy's, but he finally looked up. "Are you calling it a day?"

"I am. I have a client in my Santa Monica office, and then I'm heading home." She hoped Jake got her meaning that she'd be ready to go to the library with him, without blurting it out in front of Billy. It was one thing for Billy to know about their budding relationship, if that was what you could call it, and another to flaunt the fact that she and Jake were working on a sideline to the case.

She could handle just one person at a time finding out that she'd stabbed her foster dad to death.

Jake winked at her. "Have a good session. Is that what you therapists say?"

"No, never. Have a nice evening. I'll see you two tomorrow. Hope you get a hit on that print."

"Ditto." Jake held up his hands, crossing the fingers of both.

Kyra made the drive home toward the coast, antsy to drop by Quinn's house to let him know she'd taken his advice and told Jake about her past. Quinn would also want the details on 2.0's latest murder, but Jake could serve him those details better than she could, detective to detective.

The fact that Quinn approved of and liked Jake thrilled her. If Jake met Quinn's high standards, then she knew she could trust Jake—and she could. Jake hadn't backed away from her when he found out about Buck Harmon; nor had he gotten mad at her for keeping it a secret from him.

Jake came across trauma like hers every day at his job. He'd been a homicide detective for almost ten years. Other people's misery had soaked into his bones by now, and he hadn't reached saturation point yet.

Maybe that was why the murder of those two African American women had hit Billy so hard. He'd been soaking it all in, just like Jake, but those deaths in particular had pushed him to saturation because of his missing sister.

She snorted and pulled into the parking space for

her office. She was guilty of analyzing both detectives without even seeing them professionally—not that she could ever take on Jake as a client now, and not that he would ever seek out help.

He'd had an incident with a former coworker of hers, Lizbeth Kruger. Lizbeth had submitted a report to the parole board on a killer Jake had locked up, allowing for his early release. The guy had killed again, and when Jake found out, he went ballistic on Lizbeth at the station. Kyra had missed the fireworks, but Jake's towering rage had earned him a reprimand and mandatory anger-management sessions. She could only imagine how that went.

As a result, Jake had no fondness for therapists, but he seemed to be coming around where she was concerned. That thought put a little smile on her lips that she couldn't erase until she sat down with her client, who had just lost his job and whose wife had left him because of it.

When the fifty-minute session ended, Kyra checked her phone and saw the text from Jake that they had a meeting with one of the librarians at 7:30 p.m. She recorded notes from the session on her laptop, left a note for her office mate, Candace, and drove home.

After she threw together a quick pasta dish, it took her twenty minutes to decide to leave on her work clothes instead of changing into something more casual. Jake would still have his suit on, and she didn't want the librarian to think she didn't have a right to view that footage.

Jake had indicated he'd pick her up, and they'd

go to the library together. She'd told him to text her when he was out front and started pacing at 7:05 p.m. Ten minutes later, her doorbell rang.

She squinted through the peephole and sighed at Jake standing there holding Spot. She yanked open the door. "You didn't have to walk all the way up here, and you certainly didn't need to pick up Spot. He's gonna get white cat hair all over your suit."

Jake unceremoniously dumped the cat on the ground and brushed off his slacks. "Little cat hair never hurt anything."

"Your partner would be shocked to hear that. Do you think Billy would ever allow a cat to shed on his suit?"

"Billy has two small children. When he's with his boys, he's a mess. Don't let him fool you." He nudged Spot with his foot as the cat curled his body around Jake's ankles. "And I'm not going to call for you at the curb."

She peered at him through narrowed eyes. "Did you park illegally again? Because I know for a fact there's no parking out there at this time of night."

He cleared his throat. "I may have squeezed in too close to a fire hydrant. Do you want to stand here talking about cat hair, Billy and parking, or do you want to get to the library and find out who play… La Prey is?"

"Let me grab my purse." She eased the door closed to keep Spot out and picked up her purse from the counter. Jake was right. Now that the moment had come to find out who'd been tormenting her, she was dragging her feet. She felt light-headed, as her fright-or-flight response kicked in.

When she opened the door, Jake had Spot in his arms again. "He's just doing that because he wants to be fed."

"Aw, I thought it was because he liked me."

When the door closed with a snap, Spot leaped out of Jake's arms and stalked away with a swish of his tail.

Kyra laughed. "He knows he's out of luck."

Her mouth dry on the short drive to the library, Kyra kept licking her lips and fidgeting with the strap of her purse.

Jake parked his vehicle and shot her a glance. "This is a good thing. It's going to be okay. This will help us get to the bottom of a lot of things, and I'm convinced it's going to shed light on these copycats. Hold on to that idea."

She dropped her chin in a jerky nod. She was less convinced than Jake that whoever was taunting her had knowledge about the copycat killers, but the thought gave her resolve.

Marching into the library next to Jake with a subpoena in his pocket, Kyra drew back her shoulders, feeling a confidence she had lacked the previous time she'd sidled in here with her lies about a stalker.

She just hoped Inez wasn't working the night shift.

When they entered through the glass doors, Jake veered left toward the circulation desk as opposed to the reference desk, and Kyra blew out a tiny breath from between her lips.

She hung back as Jake gave his name, flashed his badge and asked for Renee. Now, *that* was how you got results.

A short woman with chin-length dark hair streaked with gray approached the counter. "Detective McAllister, I'm Renee Shelton. I've been able to cue up the video from the date and time in question. Do you want to come around to the back?"

Jake shook hands with Renee and introduced her to Kyra. They both circled the long counter and met Renee at the end where she pulled open a swinging half door for them to step through.

As she led them to the back, she glanced over her shoulder. "I set up the computer in the office. Do you need me there to work it, or would you prefer to look at it on your own?"

Jake answered, "As long as it's cued up where we need it, I can handle the rest."

Renee ushered them into a small office with a computer set up on a table, two chairs in front of it. "I'll leave you to it, then. Let me know if you need any assistance."

They pulled the chairs up to the computer and Kyra sat on Jake's left, as he placed his hand over the mouse. "This is perfect. The cameras are pointing right at the public computers."

Kyra stared at the familiar setup of the computers, all empty now. She jabbed her finger at the workstations. "Do we know which one it is, specifically?"

"I passed the info you gave me from Brandon to the library, and Renee indicated it's the computer at the end. He should be showing up anytime now."

Kyra watched the flickering images of other people coming and going in the library, even sitting down at the public computers. She sat up when she saw Yolanda, the homeless woman from the day before, sprint toward the computers, her Santa Monica College sweatshirt bunched up around her waist. From the way she was moving, she wasn't as old as Kyra had imagined before. The sun had damaged her skin, aging her beyond her years.

"That woman was there the other day." Kyra sucked in a breath as Yolanda sat at the computer they were watching, her bags over her shoulder, a piece of paper clutched in her hand. "She must leave before La Prey gets there. Maybe he kicked her off that computer."

She hunched forward, her eyes watering as she focused on Yolanda clicking away on the keyboard, most likely bringing up articles on fashion. The minutes ticked by. Kyra's gaze darted to the clock in the upper-right corner of the video, the seconds racing.

Jake sat back in his chair and clasped his hands between his knees.

Kyra shot a glance at him, and he was no longer looking at the video.

She said sharply, "What?"

"That's it, Kyra. That's who sent you the email."

"It can't be." She cranked her head back and forth between the lying computer and Jake's grim face. "I met that woman. She's not all there. Why would she be sending me emails with the Harmon picture?"

"It's obvious, isn't it?"

"Not to me." But it was, and her stomach knotted.

"He paid Yolanda to send that email to cover his tracks. Player played us…again."

Chapter Fourteen

Kyra's cheeks flushed red, hot with anger, and she smacked her hand on the table next to the computer. "No! I met that woman. I talked to her. She couldn't have done it."

"Why? Because she's a little spacey?" Jake grabbed the mouse again and backtracked to the moment Yolanda sat down at the computer. "Look at her hand. She has a piece of paper. Those could've been her instructions."

Kyra sucked in her bottom lip and drummed her fingers on the edge of the keyboard.

"What?" Jake's word had a sharp edge, but from the look on her face, Kyra remembered something.

"When I first met her, she told me she worked at the library and people paid her for information. I gave her a twenty just to talk to her…and because I felt sorry for her." She kicked the table with the toe of her shoe. "Damn, and all this time she knew."

"That's the good news." Jake circled Yolanda's face with his finger. "She's obviously a regular here.

We'll find her, talk to her, pay her if necessary and discover who hired her."

Kyra slumped in her seat, her chin dropping to her chest. She said in a low voice, "I thought tonight was the night. I thought I'd see his face."

"We'll find him." Jake squeezed the back of her neck lightly. "That woman, Yolanda, is not going to have any loyalty to some guy off the street who paid her to send an email."

"She's not going to have any loyalty to us, either, unless I can convince her I'm a supermodel."

"Excuse me?"

"Oh—" she waved her hand in the air "—never mind. It's a long story. How are we going to locate Yolanda?"

Jake gave Kyra a quick, appraising look. She wouldn't have to do much to convince *him* she was a supermodel with her high cheekbones and wide eyes.

He dragged his gaze away from Kyra's perfect features, ended the video and closed out of the program. "You said she's a regular, right?"

"Seemed to be. The reference librarian knew her name, and Yolanda knew the reference librarian."

Jake wheeled his chair back from the desk and said, "We'll ask Renee the name of the reference librarian who usually works at the time you were here, and have her give us a call the next time she sees Yolanda."

"We don't even have to go through all that. The reference librarian who knows Yolanda is named Inez. We can tell Renee to have Inez call us…you."

"That'll work." He placed his hands on the back of her chair, his knuckles skimming her shoulder blades.

Being cooped up in this small space, working closely with Kyra, had put his senses on high alert. Every time she shifted in her chair, he caught a whiff of her rose scent. Every time her fingers accidentally brushed his hand, he felt a quiver down his spine. Despite his attraction to her, he was ready to call it a night—alone.

"What's wrong?"

Kyra had folded her arms and was bouncing her knee up and down. "How did he know that I'd track him to the library? This guy not only used a public computer, he paid someone to do the deed so he wouldn't be caught on camera."

"He's not an amateur." Jake lifted his shoulders. "He knew to contact Matt Dugan, used Matt's knowledge of you to stalk you. He knows you work with the police because he left one of the cards by your car parked outside the station. He knows who you are, Kyra. That's no secret."

She hopped up suddenly. "And we're going to know who he is soon enough."

They exited the room and Jake poked his head into the office next door. "Renee, we're done, but we do have another request."

"Did you find what you were looking for?"

"In a manner of speaking." Jake slid a glance at Kyra. "We'd like to speak to a homeless person who was on the computer. Kyra said that the reference librarian, Inez, knows who she is."

Renee gave them a tight smile. "That doesn't surprise me. Inez would know the regulars on the public computers."

Jake raised his eyebrows hopefully and asked, "Is
Inez here tonight?"

"Inez left for the day. If you want to leave your
card, I can have her call you."

Kyra rustled in her purse. "I'd like to leave my
card with a note for Inez. I met her yesterday, and
she'll know what I'm talking about."

"That's fine." Renee held out a pen to Kyra, who
continued to rummage in her purse.

"Thanks." Kyra leaned over Renee's desk and
printed a note on the back of one of her cards. Before
she handed it to Renee, she nudged Jake in the ribs.
"Leave one of your cards with mine so she knows
it's part of the search warrant and legit."

Jake pulled a card out of his pocket and handed it
to Kyra, who held them out to Renee.

"I will leave these for Inez at the reference desk
so she can't miss them."

They both thanked Renee and walked out into
the night air, now being taken over by a low marine
layer rolling in from the Pacific.

Jake stopped under a streetlamp that had just
turned on, the moist air carrying a hint of salt and
caressing his face. "What was in the note?"

"I told her I needed to speak with Yolanda and to
let me know the next time she saw her in the library,
or at least let me know the hours Yolanda haunted
the public computers." She shook her head, her blue

eyes glassy beneath the light. "I'm just not sure how much help Yolanda's going to be. She thinks she's involved with the fashion industry and that she's looking for new styles for the designers."

Jake pressed a hand to his forehead. "Wow. How did The Play...La Prey manage to settle on Yolanda for this task? Seems like he was taking a big risk with her."

Kyra jerked her head up when he almost said The Player again. He'd honor her wishes of calling the guy La Prey in her presence, but that didn't change the fact that he'd used an anagram of the player to ID himself.

She brushed her hair from her face, accustomed to having it drawn into a ponytail. "Yolanda must have her moments of clarity, or maybe she's just really good at following directions."

"We'll find out, one way or the other." Jake turned toward where he'd parked his car, and after a few moments, Kyra followed him.

As he opened the door for her, he grabbed her hand. "Didn't Quinn ever tell you that good investigative work takes time?"

Her lips lifted at one corner. "Quinn also told me to trust you. I should always listen to Quinn."

Jake slammed her door with a full-fledged smile on his face. He owed Quinn a six-pack.

THE NEXT MORNING, Jake walked into the task force war room, dragging his heels. Castillo had already called him to let him know he was going out to

Mindy Behr's family home today in San Marino, a ritzy area just south of Pasadena.

Turned out the Behrs were big contributors to Mayor Wexler's campaign. Now the brass would turn up the heat even higher on the task force. The urgency of the investigation shouldn't depend on the victims, but it often turned out that way.

His eyes tracked to Kyra's desk as if it held some magnetic power over him—just like she did—but she hadn't made it in yet. She didn't always report to the station to work. She had clients outside her police work, although he knew she was one of the LAPD-sanctioned therapists. Her name had even cropped up on the list the department had handed to him when they mandated anger-management sessions for him after his blowup at that Lizbeth woman.

He'd opted out of one-on-one therapy and had chosen a group meeting instead. He had to admit the group had helped him, but it was because the group leader, Max Darotta, employed what Jake learned later was behavioral therapy. Max gave the group members actual tools to use. He couldn't have handled sitting there talking about his feelings.

He gave a shiver and hunched his shoulders. It was a good thing he hadn't chosen therapy with Kyra after all. At that time he probably would've hated it and her, and then he wouldn't have been able to date her later.

Not that they'd been on an actual date yet.

He jumped as Billy thumped his back. "Daydreaming, brother?"

"Yeah, daydreaming about when you're going to come up with some video we can actually use."

"Just might be your lucky day." Billy winked and then hunched in closer. "You hear the Behr family is connected?"

"Friends of Wexler's. Castillo called me this morning. I'm taking a jaunt out to San Marino today to talk to them."

Billy crossed one index finger over the other and held them out. "I can't go with you today. Is that all right, or does Castillo expect the both of us?"

"Hate to break it to you, Billy, but your name never came up in the conversation."

"Then you're on your own." Billy skimmed his hand across his short Afro. "This is a PR move for Castillo and Chief Sterling. From what I've heard, Mindy didn't have much contact with her parents. They didn't know her friends, but it didn't stop them from disapproving of them. They're not going to be able to tell you much about Mindy's habits and whether or not she was being stalked."

"I know that, but you're a better PR guy than I am."

"You're the task force lead." Billy drilled his finger into Jake's chest. "They want the top dog."

Jake barked just as his desk phone rang. "McAllister."

"It's Captain Castillo. You're taking Kyra with you to the Behrs."

Jake's heart jumped and then settled to a dull thud. Though he looked forward to any time spent with

Kyra, it wasn't common for someone like her to sit in with a detective when he or she was questioning family members. Now he knew Billy was right. This was a PR move.

"You got a problem with that? I thought you two were—" Castillo cleared his throat "—getting along."

Jake hadn't been too pleased with Kyra's appointment when they'd first formed the task force for the Copycat Player. He'd moved past that...way past that.

"No problem at all, Cap. I've watched her work, and she's an asset. I'm just wondering what kind of interview this is going to be. Do the parents have material evidence or insight into their daughter's murder?"

Castillo snapped. "No. Wexler and the chief are calling the shots on this one and the rest of us dance. Is that too hard for you to figure out, J-Mac?"

Jake had held the receiver away from his ear and now rolled his eyes at Billy, who was mouthing something to him.

"No, sir. Not at all. I'll let Kyra know, and we'll be out there this afternoon."

Castillo slammed the phone down before Jake could even pull the receiver from his ear. "What is Castillo's problem these days? He acts like we never ID'd and stopped the Copycat Player last month."

"You know how it goes." Billy raised his eyes to the ceiling, holding his palms up. "Stuff rolls downhill. Wexler's on Sterling's backside, who's on Castillo's backside, who's on ours. We just need to find a way to remove a few of those backsides."

"Thanks for the primer on politics." Jake folded his hands behind his head. "Now give me one on handling well-connected families of victims, who are probably going to report back to the chief."

"You don't need me for that. You'll have Kyra with you. She'll have your back, but you know what?" Billy's gaze wandered to Kyra's side of the room. "You might want to watch that one."

Jake's pulse ticked at the side of his mouth. Had Billy discovered something about Kyra's past? "What do you mean?"

"She saw Tara's name on your phone, and then she hit me up later and asked if you were dating Tara. Bro, you don't want no crazy girlfriend. They become crazy *ex*-girlfriends."

Jake let out a breath that turned into a chuckle. He *wished* Kyra was the jealous type. "I think she's okay. Haven't seen her today?"

"No." Billy waved at two cops coming through the door. "We've got video to look at. We got a line on some cars in Andrea's neighborhood, and a few of them look similar to cars in Crystal's neighborhood. We're going to isolate those and get to work on the blocks around Mindy's house."

"Thank God for CCTV." When Billy walked away, Jake picked up his work cell and called Kyra. She answered right away.

Her voice breathless, she asked, "Did Inez from the library call you?"

"Haven't heard from her yet, but it's still early." He paused as Kyra breathed heavily into the phone. "Are you okay?"

"I'm fine. Just finished doing some yoga on my living room floor."

His heart returned to its regular beats per minute, which were higher than normal when talking to Kyra anyway. "The task force has an assignment for you."

"I know. Captain Castillo already called me. I can be at the station in about ninety minutes if that's not too late."

"I'll make sure it's not. I haven't even called the Behrs yet to set a time. Not that I'm complaining, but do you know how this came about? How did they even know we had someone like you on the task force?"

"No clue. Maybe they were asking for additional services? People like that are accustomed to full-service attention—not that I'm saying they don't deserve it at this time."

"Just curious. I'll see you at the station in an hour and a half, then. Good thing I wore one of the suits Billy suggested for me."

"You may not have the sartorial splendor of Billy, but you can definitely fill out a suit."

When they ended the call, Jake had a warm feeling in the pit of his stomach at Kyra's compliment. He really didn't want a jealous woman—he'd seen how deadly that emotion could be—but could puff out his chest a little at Kyra's compliment. If she wanted him for more than his detective's mind, he'd take it.

The warm fuzzies receded as he pondered the puzzle of Kyra Chase. She seemed to have connections he could never quite fathom, and he didn't know why those connections always came with an edge of mystery.

DRAGGING THE ELASTIC band from her hair, Kyra muttered to herself, "Definitely fill out a suit? You are definitely an idiot. Who says things like that?"

She rolled up her yoga mat and shoved it into the hall closet. On the phone with Jake, she'd had an urge to step up her game. He hadn't made any moves last night when they left the library, but then she hadn't exactly been sending out welcoming vibes.

She'd been angry when she discovered La Prey had beat her again. Seeing his image on the library video and identifying him would've put an end to his torment. What did he want from her, anyway? He hadn't demanded money or information or favors. Probably one of those sick crime buffs who spent all his time researching other people's misery and wanted to feel connected to it all. She knew there were internet discussion groups, blogs and message boards devoted to true crime. She'd snuck in on a few of them anonymously. Some comprised amateur sleuths who cared for victims and really did want to help, and others were composed of vicarious thrill-seekers who wanted to feel close to the action. If any of them actually did get close to a violent murder, they'd change their minds really fast and find another hobby.

As she showered, she heard Jake's lingering questions in her head. She had an idea how she'd gotten on the Behrs' radar. Mindy Behr's mother must be friends with Monica Wexler, the mayor's wife. Even if Kyra would never reveal that she saw Monica Wexler on a professional basis, there was nothing stopping Monica from telling her friends about her therapist.

Jake could continue to think she had some Svengali-like powers over the LAPD, or that Quinn's influence somehow stretched to the mayor's office, but she'd never out a client. Everyone had a right to their secrets.

Dressed in a pair of straight-legged beige slacks and a white blouse with a ruffle at the neck, Kyra draped a beige sweater with a white zigzag through it over her shoulders and locked up her apartment.

On her drive to the station, she checked her phone several times for a message or call from Inez. She'd also kept an eye out for Yolanda on her morning walk down to the beach and back, peering at transients on bus stop benches and huddled on the steps of businesses before they opened for the day. Other than a few requests for money and an invitation to go swimming in the ocean, she had come up empty. Yolanda could spend her nights in a shelter and then wander into the library during the day to do her...business.

Kyra eased out a sigh and rolled into the parking lot of the LAPD's Northeast Division. She'd have to leave the finding of Yolanda to Inez.

When she got to the conference room that housed

the task force, she stood at the door with her mouth slightly ajar as she watched the activity and heard a buzz of conversation. Grabbing the sleeve of one of the uniforms as he squeezed past her, she said, "Fingerprint?"

"Video."

Kyra wended her way to Jake's desk and planted herself next to it. "You have promising video?"

"A couple of cars from Andrea's neighborhood around the time we figure someone snuck into her garage match a couple of cars in Crystal's neighborhood. We have clear enough footage on Andrea's tape to get some license plates. Billy and his team are scouring the footage in Mindy's neighborhood." Jake grabbed his jacket and grimaced. "And I have to leave the action to hold the hands of Wexler's pals."

"Hey!" Kyra jabbed him in the ribs. "Wexler's pals are also grieving parents. They can't help it if they have the pull to get some extra attention. Anyone in their position would take advantage of that."

"You're right." He put a hand over his heart. "That's why you're going with me."

Herding her out of the room with his hand pressed to the small of her back, Jake pointed at Billy and said, "Keep me posted."

Kyra didn't mind the heads turning at their departure. They had a legitimate reason to be together today.

As Jake took his car north through LA to the Foothill Freeway, they discussed the case, Yolanda and even Billy's canceled meeting with the PI today. Kyra wasn't the only one tiptoeing around their mutual decision last night to head to their own beds, alone.

Whenever the time seemed to be right and their emotions swept them up in a tidal wave, some outside force erected a barrier, or, in the case of the phone call from Jake's daughter, the force was more like an insinuation that floated between them.

Last night the only emotions Kyra could muster were anger and frustration at the wiliness of her adversary, and Jake had seemed tired, defeated. Did he feel as if he had to work too hard at seduction? Would he get tired of the effort?

She focused her gaze outside the window at the banners with roses on them as they followed the same route as the Rose Parade. Tapping the glass, she said, "I always wanted to go to the Rose Parade when I was a kid. Did you ever go?"

He snorted. "My old man would've never taken us to anything like that, but I've been a few times as an adult with Fiona. Even camped out one night on the sidewalk."

"That's dedication." Jake didn't sound like such a horrible dad to her. She took a deep breath to ask him more about his childhood, only knowing his dad had been a cop, too, but Jake whistled and gestured out the window.

"We're going to start heading into the nice area now."

"The whole area looks nice to me."

"Wait until we go past the Huntington Library toward Lacy Park. That's where the Behrs are."

"Leave it to Wexler to cultivate friends in high places." She didn't need her client Monica Wexler to tell her about the mayor's ambition, which was one of the sticky points in their marriage. Everyone in LA knew the mayor had his sights set on bigger and better prizes.

As Jake turned down the Behrs' street, Kyra wrinkled her nose at the stately mansions a discreet distance from each other, sporting golf-course-worthy lawns with velvety-green grass even at the end of one of the hottest summers on record.

"I don't know. In the realm of multimillion-dollar homes, I prefer yours and Quinn's to these show-offs."

Jake gave a short bark of a laugh that sounded very much like Quinn's. "Neither Quinn's nor my house can compare with these."

"Maybe not pricewise, but your houses have these beat in character."

Jake pulled into the circular driveway of a white mansion, the blandness of it relieved by a riot of colorful flowers bordering the house and running up either side of a long walkway that cut through the grass. It all looked too cheerful for the visit.

When Jake cut the engine, Kyra put a hand on his arm. "Remember, they aren't suspects. This isn't a typical interview."

"Got it." He pinched her knee. "Have I told you I'm glad you're here?"

Kyra tried to wipe the smile off her face as they walked up the two steps to the double doors. The doorbell they pressed rang deep inside the house. Kyra almost expected a butler in tails to answer its call.

When a petite woman with fluffy blond hair opened the heavy door, Kyra blinked at her.

Straightening his jacket, Jake said, "Mrs. Behr?"

A smile touched her lips and she dabbed her red nose with a tissue. "That's right. You must be Detective McAllister, and you're Kyra Chase."

Jake stiffened beside Kyra, and she held her breath, hoping that Mrs. Behr wouldn't blurt out how she knew her name.

"That's right. I'm sorry for your loss, ma'am."

"Thank you, Detective." She stepped to the side and widened the door. "Please come in and join us on the patio. You can remove your jacket, Detective. It's cool enough in the back, but it feels like we're having one of those extended summers, doesn't it?"

"It sure does, ma'am, especially with the Santa Ana winds last month and those wildfires blazing."

Mrs. Behr, looking crisp in white capris, a blue-and-white polka-dot blouse and white sandals, led them through a great room that opened onto the patio. A pocket wall had been fully retracted so that there was no division at all between the inside of the house and the outside except for a track on the floor that separated the wood of the great room from the pavers on the patio.

Okay, maybe this was a little nicer than Quinn's beach cottage on the Venice canals.

As they stepped onto the patio, Mr. Behr rose

from a chair, shunting his laptop to the side and running a hand through his thinning hair, where the salt was beginning to take over the pepper.

"Darling, this is Detective McAllister and Kyra Chase. She's the—"

Mr. Behr interrupted his wife. "I know who she is. I'm Michael Behr. Thank you for coming."

Jake shook Mr. Behr's hand. "I'm sorry for your loss, Mr. Behr. We're doing everything we can to catch Mindy's killer."

A jagged sob escaped from Mrs. Behr's lips, and Kyra launched forward and took her arm. "Let's sit down."

Mr. Behr motioned Jake into a chair.

"We don't want special treatment, you know. That was the mayor's idea. There were two other victims before Mindy, and I'm sure you didn't make personal visits to their homes." He peered up at Jake from his clasped hands.

"We're always available to talk to all of the victims' families, and Kyra is part of the task force and on call if anyone, even the detectives, needs to talk."

"Th-that's nice." Mrs. Behr crumpled her tissues in her fingers. "Really, we just want an overview of the investigation. Surely, that's something you can share with all the families, can't you?"

She shot her husband a look from beneath wet lashes, and he set his jaw.

It was clear who had arranged for this meeting. Mrs. Behr may have even gotten the idea from Monica Wexler, who in turn encouraged her husband to reach out.

Jake sat forward in his chair. "We can absolutely tell you the status of the investigation—up to a point. Certain things we keep from the press and even the families, if we feel those things will help us solve the case faster. Does that make sense?"

"It does," Mr. Behr answered as he waved his hand at someone in the great room.

A short Latina with worried eyes and her own tissue crumpled in her hand scurried out to the patio. "Yes, Mr. Michael?"

"Elena, could you please bring us some drinks?" Mr. Behr's gaze darted between Jake and Kyra. "Lemonade, iced tea, both?"

Kyra smiled at Elena. "I'll take a lemonade, please."

"Same, thank you." Jake nodded at Elena, who didn't ask what Mr. and Mrs. Behr wanted.

This kind of money secured you workers who probably knew your needs before you did.

When Elena disappeared, Jake launched into an overview of where the LAPD stood on the case. He included the detail of the playing card between the lips, but left off the severed finger. The families would learn about that indignity later when they got back their loved ones' bodies for burial or cremation.

Jake did a good job of sanitizing the descriptions, and he trailed off when Elena came back with a tray of four tall glasses filled with pale yellow liquid with ice tinkling inside like delicate wind chimes.

When he resumed his narrative, punctuated by questions from the Behrs, Kyra noticed he also declined to mention the latest development with the video. Didn't want to give false hope or just didn't want news getting out yet.

When he wound up, Kyra started her job. She asked the Behrs questions about Mindy and encouraged them to talk about her—not to help the investigation but to help themselves. They hadn't had two seconds to grieve, and they needed to start that process.

Mrs. Behr was the one who ended the meeting by putting her glass aside and shifting in her seat. "We appreciate your visit so much, don't we, Michael?"

Jake's thorough discussion of the investigation had brought Mr. Behr around, and he also seemed to understand how important it was for his wife.

By the time she and Jake got back to his car, Kyra felt drained, as if she'd just facilitated a two-hour group session. She collapsed in the passenger seat, leaned her head back and closed her eyes. "I'm exhausted."

Jake tapped her shoulder, and she opened one eye, focusing on the phone he held out to her. "What?"

"Too tired to drive out to Santa Monica and talk to Yolanda?"

She bolted upright in her seat and scrambled for her own cell phone. "Inez called you?"

"Almost right after we sat down with the Behrs and I turned off my phone." He squinted at it now.

"About two hours ago. Said Yolanda was at the library."

Kyra's fingers closed around her phone, and she pulled it free from her purse. "She texted me, too. Same thing. Let's hurry. We might catch her in the library."

Jake put on the speed, but traffic wouldn't cooperate. Kyra had put in a call to Inez, who hadn't responded yet.

As they got off the freeway and veered onto Lincoln, Inez returned Kyra's call. "I'm sorry. Yolanda just left. I sent you and the detective texts as soon as I saw her here."

Kyra made a face at Jake. "Thank you for that. Do you know which direction she was headed? Do you know where she stays at night?"

"I think she stays at the women-only shelter in downtown LA sometimes, but not always. When she leaves the library she sometimes goes down to the pier to get food from the restaurants there."

"Thanks, Inez. We'll try that, or we can catch her another day."

"She hasn't done anything wrong, has she?"

"Not at all. We just want to talk to her about someone she might have met. Have you ever seen her talking to a man in the library?"

"Yolanda will talk to anyone who talks to her, but I've never noticed anyone in particular."

"Okay, I'll let you know if you need to keep a lookout tomorrow, too."

Jake idled at a stop sign. "Let's try for another

day. We're so close to your place. If you don't need anything from the station, I can just drop you off at home and take you back in the morning."

Kyra turned her head to look at his slightly flushed face. Did he mean he'd drive all the way back to his place in West Hollywood after dropping her off and then come back in the morning to pick her up? Or did he mean he'd spend the night and the two of them would go into the station together?

She broke off as the wail of a siren swooped down on them from behind.

"Whoa." Jake rolled forward a little bit and veered to the right to clear the way for the ambulance and cop car.

Kyra stared at a crowd of people up ahead on the corner of Ocean, across the street from the pier, and her heart pounded in her chest. "Inez mentioned that Yolanda sometimes went to the pier after the library to scrounge for food. Let's look there first before giving up today."

"Okay, but in case you haven't noticed, it's kind of a mess up there." His hands resting on top of the steering wheel, Jake pointed at the clutch of people and emergency vehicles.

"You're in your LAPD car. When have you ever shied away from parking this thing illegally?" She waved a finger at a red curb in a bus lane ahead and to the right. "Stop over there. I want to see what's going on. I have a bad feeling about this."

"About this?" He nodded at the scene on the corner.

"Yeah. Just humor me."

The sedan lurched forward into the intersection and cruised to a stop on the red curb that would give anyone else a ticket in a minute flat.

Before Jake even cut the engine, Kyra had the door open and was scrambling from the car. As Jake called after her, she broke into a jog and hung on the edge of the crowd clumped around an accident scene in the street.

Her breath catching in her throat, she asked everyone and no one in particular, "What happened?"

"Car versus pedestrian."

"Hit and run."

"Some homeless lady."

"Think she's dead."

With her head swimming and the blood pounding against her temples, Kyra shimmied and ducked through the lookie-loos until she staggered to the front, bordering the street.

A body, already covered with a white sheet, lay in the street. One edge of the sheet had flipped back, and in the revolving red and blue lights, Kyra could make out the logo for Santa Monica College on the dirty gray sweatshirt.

Chapter Fifteen

Jake ran to catch up with Kyra and, peering over the crowd, could see her blond head. What the hell was she doing gaping at the scene of a hit and run?

He cupped his hand around his mouth and yelled, "Kyra!"

He had to try a second time before her head whipped around, and he staggered back at eyes as big as saucers on her face and her mouth open in a perfect O. She looked like she'd seen a ghost.

She turned her body in his direction and battled the crowd to reach him.

She fell against him heavily. He wrapped one arm around her and pulled her close to his chest, where he felt her heart hammering against him.

"What is it? What happened?"

She planted her hands against his chest and looked up into his face, whispering, "It's her."

He glanced at the uniforms doing crowd control and the ambulance parked at an angle in the middle of the street. "Yolanda? You're telling me that the hit-and-run victim is Yolanda?"

"Yes." She grabbed the front of his shirt, nearly ripping it off his body. "He did it. I know he did it. He took care of Matt, too. Think about it."

"Slow down a minute." He had to practically drag her away from the scene. Amid the chaos, nobody even noticed their drama. "Sit here."

He'd pushed her into a plastic chair at a fast-food restaurant's outdoor patio. A number of patrons had already abandoned their food and tables to get a look at the accident scene.

"How do you know that's Yolanda? As far as I could see, the body had already been covered."

"Not completely. The sheet had hitched up on one side and I saw her clothing."

"You recognized the clothing of a homeless person you saw once?" He didn't want to believe her, didn't want to face the consequences of her truth, and was throwing everything he had at her.

"It was distinctive." She grabbed the straw stuck in a drink and, with her lips puckered, pulled it toward her until he slid the cup away from her.

"That's not your drink."

She blinked and released the straw. "She was wearing a gray sweatshirt from Santa Monica College. I noticed it because I teach classes there sometimes. Yolanda went on about working in the fashion world, so, of course, I checked out her clothes. The woman lying dead in the street is wearing the same sweatshirt."

The corner of Jake's eye started twitching, and he smacked himself on the side of the head to stop it. "You think La Prey had something to do with Yolanda's death."

It wasn't even a question. Of course Kyra thought that. Didn't he?

Ignoring her tilted head and pursed lips, he plowed on. "What were you saying about Matt?"

"When you set up that meeting with Matt at the motorcycle shop in Van Nuys, he was going to tell you who paid him off to plant the cards for me, wasn't he?" She folded her hands, trapping her fidgety fingers.

"I think he was also planning to tell me that you'd killed Buck Harmon. I mentioned he had dirt on you. I didn't suspect *you* of killing Matt."

"Didn't you?" She raised her eyebrows at him and then grabbed a French fry.

He slapped her hand. "Those aren't yours."

"Ugh." She pushed the half-eaten food away from her. "Matt is about to reveal information to you about La Prey and he dies of a drug overdose, which is not a surprising way for him to go out. Yolanda might tell us who paid her to send me that email and she dies in a hit-and-run accident, which wouldn't seem too suspicious for a transient to meet her end that way. Quinn always told me…"

They recited together, "There are no coincidences in police work."

Holding up his hand, Jake said, "But was Yolanda going to tell us anything? And how would La Prey know if she was?"

"Stop being such a…detective." She flailed her

hands in the air. "How does he know anything, Jake? He just does."

He got up from the uncomfortable chair and aimed a finger at Kyra. "You stay here—and don't eat or drink anything from this table. It's not yours."

He stalked back to the accident scene, clutching his badge in his hand, and found the Santa Monica PD sergeant in charge, Campos. As way of introduction, he said, "Jake McAllister, LAPD Robbery-Homicide, Sergeant Campos. Is the victim a homeless person named Yolanda?"

The sergeant puffed up his pumped-up chest until Jake thought the buttons would pop off his uniform. "What's your interest here?"

Jake sucked a breath into his mouth and expelled it from his nose, briefly closing his eyes behind his sunglasses, grateful to the late sunsets that he still needed them. He didn't feel like getting into some kind of contest with this guy.

"I'm not interested in stepping on your turf. I had a few questions I wanted to ask Yolanda related to a homicide I'm investigating. If you could verify for me that Yolanda is the victim and give me anything you got on witnesses or the car, I'll be on my way."

This de-escalation stuff really worked. Campos seemed to deflate and ducked in toward Jake until he could smell the sergeant's cheesy cologne.

Campos replied, "No positive ID yet, but we've heard a few names and Yolanda is one of them. The car was a white SUV. We got the plates, called it in immediately, and the owner reported it stolen earlier today. Probably why the guy took off after the accident."

"Probably." Jake pressed his card into Campos's hand and said, "Impressive work. Call me if you have any more information."

Campos nodded and strode off to the call of one of his officers.

Car theft, murder. La Prey was more than a stalker. Was he a serial killer, too? No. He'd been taunting Kyra during the Copycat Player killings, and that serial killer had turned out to be barista Jordy Lee Cannon, a geek who lived at home with his mother.

When he got back to the patio of the fast-food place, a couple was sitting at the table munching their food.

"Psst." Kyra waved at him from the other side of the patio. When he joined her, she thrust a soda in his hand. "They kicked me off their table."

"They probably would've done worse if you'd eaten all their food." He sucked down some soda. "Thanks."

"What did you discover?"

"They haven't ID'd the victim yet, but the name Yolanda is floating around. They *did* ID the car already. A witness got the plates, and it's a stolen car."

She shook the ice in her cup. "I can't believe it. No, I can believe it. He's not going to get caught that easily, is he? Poor Yolanda. I wonder how he figured out she was going to rat on him."

"We don't even know if she was…and neither did

he. He could've just as easily offered her more money for keeping quiet."

"If you'd met Yolanda, you'd know that would've been a tricky proposition."

"Then he knew it, too, and killed her." Jake slurped up the rest of his drink and tossed it into the recycling bin. "I'm starving. I haven't eaten since breakfast, and that's the first drink I've had since that lemonade with the Behrs. Can I interest you in dinner?"

"We can pick up food and drop in on Quinn. I haven't told him any of these new—"

"No."

Her head jerked back and her blue eyes widened.

"As much as I like Quinn and as much as I appreciate his insight on these cases, I'm done for the day. I need to turn off my brain. I need to breathe."

A little smile haunted her lips. "That's good advice for your anger management."

"I thought that stuff was supposed to be confidential."

"I can make deductions." She patted his cheek. "Wipe that scowl off your face. I'm down with dinner for just the two of us, and I'm sure Quinn would approve."

"I seem to remember a funky steak house down on Ocean, Chez Jay. Is that still there?"

"It's still there, and I haven't been in years." She tugged on his sleeve. "We can walk from here, but you can't leave your car parked in the red forever."

They made their way through people still milling around the accident scene. Jake picked up his pace when he saw something flapping beneath his windshield wiper.

Kyra crowed. "You got a parking ticket."

Jake snatched the fluttering sheet of paper and scanned the note. He crumpled it and shoved it into his pocket. "It's not a ticket."

As he opened the passenger door for her, she raised her eyebrows at him. "What did it say?"

He grunted before answering. "'Welcome to Santa Monica. Park illegally in your own city.'"

KYRA SIPPED THE last of her red wine, its warmth cruising through her bloodstream and melting her bones. Since halfway through her second glass, she hadn't thought about Yolanda's violent death or how La Prey knew his email emissary had been discovered and was about to be questioned.

She eyed the wine bottle on the table through a pleasant fog. Jake had suggested ordering the bottle with their steaks, and he'd had less than two glasses, his second half-full, the ruby liquid shimmering in the candlelight.

Tapping his glass with her fingernail, she said, "Are you trying to get me drunk?"

"Someone has to drive. Besides, you needed it more than I did." He rubbed the back of her hand with his thumb. "Feeling better?"

"A little wine won't make it go away—not even a lot of wine."

"I know that better than most, but at least your

face has lost its pinched look and your fingers aren't busy pulling threads from the tablecloth."

"That bad, huh?"

"Understandable. Are you ready to leave?"

She swallowed and nodded, the haze lifting as she thought about the short ride back to her place in Jake's LAPD sedan, her car stuck at the station and both of them going to the same place in the morning. It only made sense for him to stay at her apartment.

"I'm ready." She dropped her napkin onto the table beside her plate.

On the drive to her apartment, Kyra shot a quick glance at Jake. She'd been the one to break things off twice before just when things had gotten interesting. She should be the one to make the first move now.

As his car crawled down her block, she realized he was actually looking for a legal parking space. That could only mean one thing—he planned to stay the night.

He parallel parked with ease and opened his door. "I'll walk you up."

Just walk her up? Did that mean he didn't intend to stay?

Suddenly she had never wanted anything more in her life than to feel Jake's body next to hers—convenience be damned, first-move protocol be damned.

For a change, she waited in the car while he came around to the passenger side like she knew he would. When he opened the car door, she got out and fell against his chest, wrapping her arms around his neck. She breathed against his warm, slightly salty skin. "You're spending the night—and I don't mean on the couch."

He put one hand on her lower back and tipped up her chin with the other. "Is that the wine talking?"

"Wine doesn't talk. This is me." She grabbed his face with both hands and planted a kiss on his mouth.

He reeled beneath her sudden assault, then recovered quickly and kissed her back until he'd sapped her strength. That wasn't the wine, either.

His arm around her and her hand grasping the front of his shirt, they staggered down the sidewalk to her apartment building, looking like a couple of drunks on a bender, but it was desire for each other, not alcohol, that fueled their intoxication. At her door, she scrabbled for her keys, dropped them and then banged heads with Jake as they both reached down to retrieve them.

This mishap ended in another soul-searing kiss at the front door, the keys forgotten on the ground between them. Spot meowed and brought them to their senses.

Rubbing the side of his head, Jake said, "Let me."

He picked up her key chain, and it took him three tries to get the key in the slot.

As she bumped open the door with her hip, she grinned and said, "I was hoping your aim would be better than that."

He chuckled, a low sound that reverberated in his chest and practically lifted her from the floor as he swept her inside, slamming the door on a grumpy Spot. "You're too sassy for your own good."

As punishment for her sassiness, he sealed his mouth over hers and pushed her against the wall in the short hallway.

If they had to stop and kiss like this every few feet before they made it to the bedroom, she wanted a preview of coming attractions. She yanked at the buttons on his shirt and freed it from his slacks. She skimmed her hands across the tight-fitting, V-necked T he had under his dress shirt, the thin material clinging to his muscles.

Pinching the material off his chest, she yanked the T-shirt from his slacks. Her hands wandered beneath the shirt and splayed across the ridges of his pecs.

His hands had been busy, too, and her blouse gaped open. His fingers skimmed the edge of her lacy bra as he kissed her throat.

He murmured against her throbbing pulse. "I need a shower."

"Not cold?"

"Definitely not cold."

"This is an old apartment. I'm not sure my shower is going to be big enough for the two of us, but we'll have to make do 'cause I'm not letting you out of my sight." She stepped back and crooked her finger at him.

He needed no more encouragement than that. He followed her into the small bathroom, dwarfing everything in it.

Kyra whipped aside the shower curtain, and the

blue mermaids hissed and sighed in response, the clacking of the shower curtain rings sounding like applause from their tiny hands.

She cranked on the water to warm it up and turned to grab Jake's belt. "Normally, people are naked when they take showers."

"That's what I'm counting on."

The two of them scrambled out of their clothes, bumping their elbows against each other and the walls in their haste.

With Jake standing naked in front of her, she ran her hands down the front of his body, stopping just shy of his erection. She tickled her fingers over the tattoo on his left arm, the tiger fully visible now.

Jake shivered and lifted her off the ground with one arm, placing her in the shower. He climbed in after and she soaped up his massive frame.

He kept grabbing her wrist to stop the exploration of her hands, and finally growled, "There's not enough room in here for what I want to do with you."

As he washed her body with his rough hands, she imagined all the disappointment, pain and horror of the day sloughing off her skin and circling down the drain.

His hands caressed her soapy breasts, sending tingles cascading through her body. She wrapped her arms around his waist to stay upright as her legs wobbled, and his erection brushed her belly.

With a groan, Jake turned off the water and grabbed a towel from the rack outside the shower.

"I forgot to get another towel for you."

"Do you have a problem with sharing? Because I plan to share a lot more than a towel with you."

He patted her dry with the towel first and then swiped it over his own body when she stepped out of the shower.

She backed up into her bedroom, where her king-size bed dominated the room. As her knees hit the edge of the bed, her stomach dipped and she covered her mouth. "I—I don't have any condoms."

He grabbed his pants from the bathroom floor and pulled his wallet from the pocket. He held up two foil squares in his fingers. "At least one of us was thinking ahead."

"Always keep some handy, do you?" She twirled a lock of her hair around her finger, relief and jealousy warring in her breast.

"Ever since I met you." He descended on her, and they fell to the bed together, a tangle of arms, legs and tongues.

As Jake made love to her body, her mind opened to him completely. He knew her. He'd scaled all her walls, stared into her face, unblinking—and he hadn't looked away.

When he entered her, she closed around him. Her tongue tasted the soap on his skin. Her fingers traced the hard muscles on his back and buttocks. She sighed against his shoulder, baring her teeth against his flesh as he drove into her.

His frame shuddered and he whispered hoarsely in her ear. "Look at me."

She turned her head and met his eyes, losing herself in the dark, murky green as his climax claimed every inch of his body…and hers.

His thrusts slowed down, and he squeezed his eyes closed as if savoring every last moment of their connection. When he rolled to her side and nuzzled her throat, she felt a profound and immediate loss.

She burrowed her head into the crook of his neck and twined her legs around his to prolong their contact. As she skimmed her hand across his damp chest, she had a moment of panic. What if he left her, too?

WITH THE SUNLIGHT streaming through the blinds the following morning and Jake still solidly by her side, Kyra took a moment to stretch her toes to the end of the bed and luxuriate in the moment, sort of like Spot after a saucer of milk.

Her head lolled to the side, and she idly stuck out the tip of her tongue to taste Jake's shoulder. Her gaze fell on the glowing digital numbers of her clock on the nightstand and she shot up.

Jake mumbled and slung a heavy arm across her waist.

"Jake!" She prodded his arm. "It's late. We slept in."

Opening one eye, he cupped her breast and toyed with her nipple. "You have someplace to be?"

She sucked in a breath and squirmed, and then she broke away from him and planted her feet on the floor. "We both do, and I'm not traipsing into the war room with you—late for all the world to see."

"I'm gonna have to wear the same clothes as yesterday, unless I have time to run home at lunch." He rubbed his eyes. "I suppose breakfast in bed is out."

"I have yogurt and granola bars if you want something quick." She twisted her head around. "Okay if I shower first?"

"Sure you don't want me to join you?" He wiggled his eyebrows up and down.

"Not if we ever hope to make it out of this apartment today." She wriggled beyond his reach as he grabbed for her.

She took a quick shower, left Jake a clean towel and returned to the bedroom to dress.

Jake was sitting on the edge of the bed, his phone to his ear, the tangled sheets pulled into his lap. He jumped up when he saw her, the sheets falling to the floor. Despite his glorious nakedness, it was his face that commanded her attention, every plane alive with excitement.

"Billy found something in the tapes?"

A wide smile claimed his lips as he nodded. "Two cars, license plates and everything, in Crystal's neighborhood, and two very similar cars in Andrea's area. Looks like we have a couple of suspects."

Chapter Sixteen

Jake sat across from the first suspect, his stomach plunging by the minute. No way was Trevor Beard their neat, anal-retentive killer. The guy couldn't even keep the doughnut crumbs from falling onto his paunch.

"So, tell me again, Mr. Beard. Why was your car in this neighborhood?" Jake drilled a finger into a still photo of Beard's car taken from a security camera a few blocks from Crystal's house.

"Like I said—" Beard took a gulp of soda and wiped the back of his hand across his mouth "—I was picking up my kid."

"At two in the morning?" Billy cocked his head and Jake could tell his partner was trying with all his might not to focus on the coffee stain on Beard's T-shirt.

"Yeah, two in the morning. My ex won't let me pick up my girl when the babysitter's there. So, I waited, and the ex didn't stumble in until around two. Figures—anything she can do to get me in trouble."

"I hear ya, brother." Billy shook his head and

whipped out the other photo, the one near Andrea's place with no clear license plate. "What about here? Is this your car?"

Beard bent over the metal desk and squinted. "I don't think so. Hard to tell. Where was it?"

Jake answered, "Canoga Park."

"No way." Beard leaned back and folded his arms on his belly. "I don't never go there."

Both Jake and Billy had already given Beard their cards.

Jake nudged Billy's foot with his own. "I think we're done here, Mr. Beard. We may call you again if we have any more questions."

"Fine by me. I didn't do nothing. Should be a crime to pick up your sleeping kid at that time of the morning, but what're you gonna do when your ex is out partying?"

"Nothing. Absolutely nothing." Billy planted his hands on the desk and pushed up. "Detective McAllister will walk you out."

Jake shot Billy a dirty look from beneath his lashes.

Beard grabbed his can. "Hey, do you have any more of those little doughnuts I can have on my way out?"

"Sure." Jake ushered Beard out the door and rolled his eyes at Billy.

When he came back, Billy was brushing crumbs from the table into his palm. "That guy would've left a trail of bread crumbs at the crime scenes."

"Yeah, not our guy."

"Which is a good thing we can eliminate him, because we got nothing, partner. No judge is going to give us a search warrant based on a car on an LA street in a video. We can't get anything from these guys."

"I'm aware." Jake slipped out of his jacket and draped it over his arm. "When's the next guy coming?"

"About fifteen minutes. He informed me that he had to leave work early for the interview."

"What's he do?"

"Engineer at an aerospace company, so basically a rocket scientist." Billy leveled a finger at the jacket. "Didn't you wear that suit yesterday?"

"I like the suit. I wore it for the visit with the Behrs and thought it would be good for the interviews." Jake shook out the jacket again to avoid Billy's eyes.

"You were late this morning, too."

"Not like I haven't been working sixteen-hour days. Who are you, my mother?"

"If I were, I'd be telling you not to spend the night at a girl's house on a school day." Billy shook his finger at Jake, and Jake displayed another finger to Billy before he walked out of the interview room.

"I'm going to grab a couple of drinks for the next guy."

Fifteen minutes later, Jake returned to the interrogation room with two sodas and a file folder tucked under one arm. He stowed the items on the table and lingered by the door. Billy had gone downstairs to meet the second suspect, or at least the man who owned the other car caught on video, and Jake always liked to watch them walk. You could tell a lot about a man by the way he walked.

Billy knew what his partner was doing and allowed the subject to walk ahead of him down the hallway.

Mr. Cyrus Fisher had good posture. He dressed his wiry frame in khaki pants with a short-sleeved light blue button-up shirt, no tie. He swung his arms at his sides, but as he approached Jake, he stuck his hands in his pockets. The crepe soles of his shoes made zero noise on the linoleum, and he inclined his head and pursed his lips when he reached the room.

Jake stuck out his hand. "Mr. Fisher, I'm Detective McAllister. Thank you for taking time out of your day to answer some questions for us."

"Certainly." He grasped Jake's hand with his own, and despite the sinewy muscles of his forearm, Fisher's grip was weak.

Jake stepped aside and gestured Fisher to the hot seat—the one bolted to the floor so that suspects couldn't turn it in a different direction. They had to face their inquisitors head-on.

Fisher eyed the other two chairs before bending his knees and lowering himself to the chair.

Jake shoved a soda across the table. "Would you like something to drink?"

"No, thank you." Fisher's sharp nose appeared sharper as he lifted his chin and peered down at the can.

"Coffee, then?"

"I never drink coffee at the end of the day, Detective McAllister." Fisher held up one bony finger. "One cup in the morning is all I allow myself."

Jake shrugged and cracked the tab on his can of soda, but his nostrils flared and his pulse ratcheted up a notch.

"No soda, no coffee. Anything else? We've got some killer doughnuts in the break room." Billy straddled the other chair.

Again, with the pained look on his face, Fisher said, "I don't eat doughnuts, Detective Crouch."

"Okay, nothing to eat or drink, then." Billy gave Fisher an appraising look. "Do you work out? You're in good shape."

Fisher allowed his thin lips to crook into a smile. "I'm a biker, Detective Crouch."

Billy slapped the desk between them with his hand. "Are you one of those guys who rides around with the bright-colored Lycra shorts? Damn, you gotta admire a man who goes out like that."

Fisher did not reward Billy with another smile. "You called me in here because you saw my car somewhere?"

"We did, Mr. Fisher." Jake flipped open the folder and with the tip of his finger dragged the photo, which showed Fisher's car caught in the vicinity of Crystal's house the morning her body was discovered, to a spot on the desk in front of Fisher.

Fisher didn't touch the photo like Beard had done. Instead, Fisher put his hands in his lap and hunched forward a little.

Billy asked, "Is that your car, Mr. Fisher?"

"Well, you know it is, Detective, because there's my license plate, clear as day and the reason why I'm here instead of finishing up work at the office."

Jake eased out a breath he'd been holding. "Can you tell us what your car was doing in that area at two in the morning?"

"Certainly I can. Can you tell me why you're asking?"

"It's near the scene of a homicide that we believe took place around that time." Jake took a sip of soda so he could hide his own face while he watched Fisher's over the rim of the can.

Fisher's expression never changed. "Terrible. My car was there because it's a shortcut I take to work sometimes."

Jake's eye twitched. Not what he was expecting.

Billy burst out with the time again. "You're going to work at two in the morning?"

Fisher tapped a badge inside his front pocket. "It's a secure building, Detective Crouch, and I work in a closed area. I'm in and out at odd times of the day. When an idea strikes, I need to act on it."

Billy gave him a look as if he were an escapee from an insane asylum, but the three of them spent the next ten minutes looking at a map that included Fisher's house, where he lived alone, the area where his car was spotted and the location of his office.

As Jake suspected, that street could be used as a shortcut. As he also suspected, Fisher's alibi would most likely check out.

When Billy sprang the second photo on him, Fisher pursed his lips again and studied the picture carefully, again never touching it. "That could be my car, but I doubt it. I don't recognize that area."

Jake said flatly, "It's Canoga Park."

"Then no. That's not my car." Fisher's gaze traveled from Jake's face to Billy's. "Is there anything else, Detectives?"

They asked him several more questions, but Fisher stuck with his original story, his cool, precise demeanor never cracking.

"All right, then." Jake stood up suddenly with a loud scrape of his chair, hoping to startle Fisher into grabbing the table or his own chair.

He didn't.

"We'll be checking with your office about the time you arrived to work that day." Billy smiled and spread his hands. "Just to dot our *i*'s and cross our *t*'s."

"Very good, Detective." Fisher made a move for the door. "I can find my way out."

"I'm sure you can, but you can understand protocol." Billy hesitated at the door to see if Fisher would grab the handle.

He didn't.

After an awkward pause of several seconds, Billy yanked open the door and Jake called after Fisher's squared shoulders. "Thanks again, Mr. Fisher."

By the time Billy came back to the interrogation room, Jake had been pacing and working up a steam.

He grabbed Billy by the shoulders. "I think that's our guy, Billy."

Billy cracked a grin. "Certainly."

"The bastard wouldn't touch a thing in here. Wouldn't leave his DNA on anything, either." Jake cocked an eyebrow at Billy. "He didn't use the men's room, by any chance, on his way out?"

"Too careful for that." Billy scratched his chin. "You know his office is going to verify his hours."

"I know that."

"We got nothing, brother."

Jake held up his hands and wiggled his fingers. "We have his print. We just need to match it to him."

KYRA SHADED HER eyes as she peered up at Jake in the parking lot of the station, the setting sun creating a glare and giving him a halo. After his performance last night, he definitely didn't deserve a halo…or maybe he did.

She coughed. "You can't just ask him for his fingerprints?"

"No. All we had was his car on a home security video in the area. The car wasn't even in front of Crystal's house, and we already verified his story with his employer. His manager confirmed that Cyrus works odd hours. They don't care as long as he puts in forty hours a week, and he usually clocks more than that. The guy's something of a genius, and they're happy to let him do what he wants. That is not enough to get his prints. He's not a suspect on paper—only in our minds."

"And he didn't leave any prints in the interview room." She chewed on her bottom lip. "Suspicious."

"Very suspicious. We've seen it before—persons of interest come in to talk and won't touch a thing. We even had a guy one time who crushed out his cigarette, bagged the butt and stuck it in his pocket, so we couldn't get his DNA when he left."

"You're rushing off now to get his prints? How do you plan to do that?"

Kyra had run into Jake in the parking lot when she'd returned to the station to grab files she'd forgotten. He'd waved her down and told her all about the rocket scientist, Cyrus Fisher. She'd been around Quinn long enough to know that cops had to trust their guts.

"I have his address."

"You said it yourself. You can't get a warrant and bust into his place. You don't have enough evidence. You don't have any evidence."

"People put their trash out, don't they? Touch the lids, toss out containers." He lifted his shoulders in the suit jacket he'd dumped on her bathroom floor and worn two days in a row, definitely looking a little worse for wear.

"You plan to skulk around in that?" She jabbed a finger at the black Crown Vic that had *police* written all over it even though it was unmarked. "He's a rocket scientist. He'll spot you in two seconds, especially if you rang any alarm bells with him by trying to get him to eat and drink in the interview room."

"I don't know if we did." Jake scratched his unshaven chin. He obviously had never made it back to his place this afternoon to freshen up after spending the whole night at her place.

"Sociopaths often think they're the smartest ones in the room, and with Cyrus's IQ, he probably believes that double. It always makes them slip up."

"Straight from the extremely kissable, luscious lips of a therapist, but I've done stakeouts before."

Her lips buzzed. "This is more than a stakeout. I'll tell you what. I'll let you use my completely non-threatening, unofficial-looking car for this adventure on one condition."

"It's not an adventure, and I already know the condition. You want to tag along."

"I deserve to tag along. What if Cyrus Fisher is La Prey? Besides," she said as she put her hand on his arm and batted her eyelashes, "this is not a dangerous mission. You're going to pick up some garbage while I drive the getaway car."

"All right. One piece of trash, and we leave." He shrugged out of his jacket and slung it over his shoulder. "Lead the way."

As Kyra traipsed to the civilian side of the parking lot, she cranked her head over her shoulder. "Why isn't Billy with you?"

"He's picking up his kids, but he knows what's going down. He had the same feeling about Cyrus as I did."

When they got into Kyra's car, Jake put Fisher's address into his phone and she started following the voice. The sun set fast as they drove east, and dusk had fallen by the time they reached Fisher's neighborhood—neat and well-ordered, just like Fisher himself, according to Jake.

They crawled toward his block and Jake said, "Damn."

She slammed on the brakes. "What's wrong?"

"Hey!" He steadied his hands against the dashboard. "Are you *trying* to call attention to your car?"

With her heart still pounding, she squeaked out, "Sorry. You startled me."

She wouldn't tell Jake this, but her nerves had started jangling, and all they were doing was retrieving a piece of trash. She couldn't imagine what it would be like to go in for an arrest.

He tapped the window. "It doesn't look like it's trash night. Nobody has bins out. I can't exactly waltz onto the guy's property and grab a flowerpot or a garden hose."

"Maybe find out when this neighborhood puts out trash and return. Do you have enough to put surveillance on him in case he goes out…hunting again?"

"Nope. We don't have the manpower for that, and I don't want him to suspect anything." He drummed his fingers on the dash. "Get closer to his address and pull to the curb. I have binoculars with me."

Kyra licked her lips as she drove onto Fisher's block. Luckily she did not have to make a U-turn to park across the street and several doors down from his tidy house with its manicured lawn.

She cut the engine, and Jake reached for his bag

in the back seat of her car, withdrawing a pair of small binoculars.

Raising them to his eyes, he said, "I just want to see what I can see."

She pulled back a little to allow him a clear view of Fisher's house.

"No trash bins and none on the side of his house, either, not that I could use that evidence anyway. Man, I don't think that guy has one twig out of place. It matches with his crime scenes."

"Is he someone you could see stalking me? Killing Yolanda?"

"No, but that doesn't mean he didn't do those things." He took a sharp breath. "He's coming out of the house."

"He is?" Kyra slumped in her seat. She could see a dark figure in the driveway of Fisher's house. "What's he doing?"

"He's leaving."

She shot up. "Jake, we have to follow him. What if he's going to plan another attack or, God forbid, kill someone?"

"Okay, okay. Easy. He's in his car."

Lights flashed in the driveway as Fisher turned on his car. Kyra ground her teeth together, hoping he didn't come this way.

Jake said, "He's going the other way. Don't start your car yet. He'll see the lights behind him. There— he turned right. Now go ahead and turn right."

Kyra started her engine and took off after Fisher's silver hybrid SUV. When she turned the corner, she could spot his headlights up ahead. "Tell me how close to get."

"You're fine. It's not too late. There are still cars coming and going in this area. He shouldn't notice anything."

She trailed behind Fisher with occasional instructions from Jake, and when the silver SUV got into the left-hand turn pocket to a major boulevard, she sighed. "That's better."

"Slow down. Don't get right behind him. Let these two cars go."

She chugged along until the two cars behind her got frustrated and wheeled around her, slipping behind Fisher's car in the pocket. Kyra stayed in the far right of her lane in case Fisher decided to study the cars behind him in his rearview mirror.

The green arrow flashed on and the car in front of her dawdled so long she almost missed the light.

Fisher's car zoomed ahead of her and then got in the right lane and slowed down.

Jake lowered the binoculars. "He's gonna park. He's gonna park."

"Where's he going?"

"I think we're in luck. There are a couple of take-out restaurants, a nail salon and a mobile phone store. I doubt he's getting his nails done or buying a cell phone."

They drove past as Fisher parked his car in the small parking lot of the strip mall.

Kyra pounded the steering wheel. "I think he just took the last spot in there."

"That's okay. We're in no hurry. Circle around the block."

She made a sharp turn around the corner and circled back around to the busy street. She turned right and slowed down.

Jake said, "Pull over to the curb ahead and idle. I'm going to see if I can look into the restaurants. I think he went into the Thai place."

She scooted into a metered parking place on the street ahead of the driveway to the strip mall parking lot. "Can you see in there?"

"His car's still here." Jake put the binoculars to his eyes, his mouth beneath screwed up at the side. "I can't get a good look. Wait!"

She clutched the steering wheel. "Do you see him?"

"Pay dirt, baby." He dropped the binoculars from his eyes, which were shining in triumph. "He's coming out of the Thai restaurant with a plate of food and a drink, and he's heading for the small patio. He's going to eat and drink and toss, and we're going to move in for the evidence."

"You're going to take it out of the trash? How will you know it's his?"

"I know he's eating from the Thai place, and we'll watch the trash can after he leaves to see who else throws something away. We got this."

They waited in the car, and Kyra's eyes burned with tears as she kept focused on the man eating from a to-go container and tapping on his computer.

She asked Jake, "What do you think he's doing on that computer?"

"He could be working, but we're going to find out when Forensics gets ahold of it. Do you know they're still not done going through Jordy's computer?"

"Finding anything on his?"

"Not that I know of, but Jordy spent a lot of hours on his laptop." He jabbed her thigh. "Here we go."

She squinted at Fisher wiping his hands on a napkin, closing his computer and bagging his trash. Her heart skipped a beat at the thought that he might take it all with him.

With the binoculars glued to his face, Jake said, "He's heading for the trash can. He's going to throw away his bag. Done."

Jake sounded like he'd been giving a play-by-play to a game and Fisher had just scored—or they had.

The sun had gone down completely, and Fisher's reverse and brake lights flashed in the parking lot as he started his car and backed out.

As he pulled out, Kyra cracked open her door and the dome light sent a pool of light into the car.

Jake told her to wait at the same time she gasped and pulled the door closed. Fisher drove past them on the other side of the street. She turned to Jake. "Do you think he saw us?"

He shrugged. "Two people in a car on a busy street. You don't need to come with me."

"Oh, yes, I do. Thai food is beginning to sound pretty good about now."

They both exited the car and marched up to the

trash can at the edge of the dining patio. Kyra hadn't taken her eyes from it and knew nobody else had put garbage in it.

Jake bent over the can with his phone and took a picture of the plastic bag. He pulled out a glove and slipped it onto his hand. Then he reached into the receptacle and pinched the handle of the plastic bag between his fingers, pulling it free.

He swung it from his gloved hand. "Got it."

He placed it on the table where Fisher had been sitting and nudged it open. "There's the container, his fork and his cup and straw. He's gotta have his prints all over this stuff."

As he stuck his camera in the bag to take more pictures, a movement to her right caught Kyra's eye. She jerked to the side and gasped as her eyes met those of Cyrus Fisher, a slight smile on his pale lips, his hand in his pocket.

"J-Jake."

Jake spun around, and his hand went to his weapon on his hip. With his eyes never leaving Fisher's face, he said, "Fisher."

"Good evening, Detective. Are you looking for something?"

Jake's hand moved to the plastic bag on the table and the crinkling noise sounded like a bomb going off in the still silence among them. "I think I found it."

"Left my prints at one of the scenes, did I?" Fisher clicked his tongue and reached for his front pocket.

Jake's fingers twitched over his weapon, but Fisher

held up a tablet. "Just a breath mint, Detective. I suppose you'll want me to do a lot of talking."

"Are you confessing now, Fisher? Because I can take you in along with your prints here."

Fisher popped the mint into his mouth and bit down on it. "I don't think so, Detective."

The blood roared in Kyra's head. She had a feeling Fisher wasn't going to come along quietly, despite his current demeanor.

Fisher chewed for a few seconds as if contemplating his choices. Then his body stiffened, and he clutched his chest.

Jake lunged forward, drawing his gun. "Stop!"

Kyra stumbled back, her hand grabbing for the back of one of the metal chairs at the table.

Fisher gurgled and dropped to his knees, his face turning purple as he gasped for breath. He fell onto his side, and his eyes rolled back as foam spewed from his lips.

"The pill! It's a suicide pill. Stop him, Jake."

Jake crouched beside Fisher, now clawing at the neck of his shirt, veins popping out on his forehead. "It's cyanide, Kyra. He's dying."

"No!" She dropped to her knees and grabbed the front of Fisher's shirt. "Why'd you do it? Why'd you copy him?"

Fisher's eyes seemed to focus for a second before his gagging ceased, and Kyra could've sworn the bastard smiled.

Epilogue

Billy kicked his feet up on his desk, tipping his chair back at a dangerous angle. "It just doesn't make any sense to me. Why would the guy off himself? He didn't even know whether or not we actually had his prints from any of the crime scenes."

"He saw me when he drove away, and must've known at that point he was in trouble."

With a lump in her throat, Kyra raised her hand, wiggling her fingers. "That was my fault. I opened the door before Fisher drove off, and my dome light attracted his attention. He didn't know me, of course, but he recognized Jake and circled back to the restaurant."

"Okay, I get why he went back to see what was up, but why the confession on the sidewalk? He didn't know what we had. He could've gone home, cleared out any evidence he had at the house and claimed he had no idea how his print wound up on that piece of tape. The DA would've required more from us than that for a big case like this."

"Billy, my man, maybe he just recognized our superior detective skills in the interview and figured he was done for." Jake kicked Billy's shoes off the desk and his chair thumped to the floor.

"Yeah, I'm sure that was it." Billy slid his jacket from the back of the chair and grabbed his laptop case. As he looked around the room, he said, "I hope this means we can finally dismantle the task force. Castillo is beaming. Chief can't stop smiling for the cameras, and Mayor Wexler is ready to hand us the keys to the city. I'm going to go home and relax for a change."

When Billy left the war room, Kyra took his chair next to Jake's and twisted her ponytail around her hand. "That was a horrible way to die, quick but far from painless. Fisher would've rather met that end than spend his life in prison? I'm with Billy. I don't understand why he did it."

"He's a killer, Kyra. Do you understand anything he did?"

"We do have profiles of serial killers. We understand a lot behind what drives them. Did the suicide pill even make sense for Fisher's personality? I'm not sure it did."

"He took it. We both saw him, and the prints we took from his trash matched the print on the tape in Mindy's bedroom. We also found the victims' locks of hair hidden in his home. He killed those women, and we had him dead to rights. Maybe he couldn't face the shame." Jake circled his finger in the air where several cops on the task force were still working, despite the fact that Fisher had died a week earlier. "I'm sure we'll find out more as we sift through the rest of his belongings. We got him. I'm just sorry he died before he could tell us anything about why he copied The Player."

"Me, too." She flicked her ponytail behind her. "Do you think Fisher was La Prey?"

"I guess we'll find out." He glanced over his shoulder at the preoccupied task force members, then leaned forward and brushed his lips across hers. "I'm sorry you didn't get your answers."

"It's almost like they don't want to be questioned, isn't it?" She twisted her fingers in her lap. "I mean, Jordy had to know you were going to shoot to kill when he tried to stab me."

"Yeah, it is." He wheeled his chair back to his own desk and started packing up. "We'd better get going if we want to pick up dinner and get to Quinn's before he falls asleep. He'll want all the latest."

She rose from Billy's chair and placed her hands lightly on Jake's shoulders. "Thanks for keeping Quinn in the loop. He loves it more than he lets on."

"I know he does." Squeezing her fingers, he whispered, "Dinner at Quinn's and then dessert at your place?"

A pulse throbbed in her throat and she purred, "Too bad we're at the station, or I'd straddle you right now."

"Now I really want to get going." Jake jumped from his chair just as Brandon Nguyen burst through the conference room door.

"I'm glad you're still here, J-Mac."

Jake rolled his eyes at Kyra. "Not for long, son. State your business."

"Oh, you're gonna want to hear this." Brandon stood at attention, clutching a folder to his chest, which looked about ready to burst.

Kyra grabbed Jake's sleeve and she didn't care who saw.

Jake's body stiffened beside her. "What did you find, Brandon?"

Brandon waved the folder in the air and crowed. "We found a connection between Jordy Lee Cannon and Cyrus Fisher. They were in contact."

* * * * *

Don't miss the next book in Carol Ericson's series
A Kyra and Jake Investigation
when The Bait *goes on sale in June 2021!*

And be sure to look for the first book in the series,
The Setup,
available now from Harlequin Intrigue!

HARLEQUIN

***Uplifting or passionate,
heartfelt or thrilling—
Harlequin has your
happily-ever-after.***

With a wide range of romance series that each
offer new books every month, you are sure to
find the satisfying escape you deserve.

Look for all Harlequin series new releases on the *last Tuesday* of each month in stores and online!

Harlequin.com

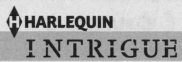
#2001 TROUBLE IN BIG TIMBER
Cardwell Ranch: Montana Legacy • by B.J. Daniels
Ford Cardwell is shocked when his college crush calls him out of the blue—
even more so when he hears a gunshot. But when he joins forces with
medical examiner Henrietta "Hitch" Rogers, she makes him wonder if he
was set up to believe the woman was a victim—not a murderer.

#2002 THE BAIT
A Kyra and Jake Investigation • by Carol Ericson
Detective Jake McAllister and victims' rights advocate Kyra Chase are
pursuing the copycat killer when the copycat kidnaps Jake's daughter, and
Kyra defies her partner to lay her life on the line. To stand a chance at survival,
they'll have to discover if this is truly a copycat...or if The Player is back.

#2003 CONARD COUNTY: TRACES OF MURDER
Conard County: The Next Generation • by Rachel Lee
As elite soldier Hillary Kristiansen and US Special Ops member
Trace Mullen bond over their grief following their shared friends' deaths,
they find themselves determined to prove that the deaths were not mere
tragedies—they were murders.

#2004 DEADLY DOUBLE-CROSS
The Justice Seekers • by Lena Diaz
Someone is trying to destroy former chief of police Mason Ford, but
he won't go down without a fight. Neither will crime scene analyst
Hannah Cantrell, who will do whatever it takes to help Mason survive.
Can Mason and Hannah discover the truth before a killer strikes again?

#2005 SHOT THROUGH THE HEART
A North Star Novel Series • by Nicole Helm
Willa Zimmerman has always known her life could be in danger. That's why,
when North Star undercover operative Holden Parker follows her home,
seeking a lead on a hit man, she captures him. But soon they learn they're
on the same side—and they're being pursued by the same foe.

#2006 UNSUSPECTING TARGET
A Hard Core Justice Thriller • by Juno Rushdan
Ten years ago, Jagger Carr saved Wendy Haas's life. Circumstances pulled
them apart, but when an assassin targets her at a charity gala, Wendy has
no choice but to trust Jagger, who's now deep undercover.

The narrow mountain road ended at the edge of a rock cliff.
It wasn't as if Ford Cardwell had forgotten that. No, when
he saw where he was, he knew it was why he'd taken this
road and why he was going so fast as he approached the
sheer vertical drop to the rocks far below. It would have
been so easy to keep going, to put everything behind him,
to no longer feel pain.

Pine trees blurred past as the pickup roared down the
dirt road to the nothingness ahead. All he could see was
sky and more mountains off in the distance. Welcome back
to Montana. He'd thought coming home would help. He'd
thought he could forget everything and go back to being the
man he'd been.

His heart thundered as he saw the end of the road coming
up quickly. Too quickly. It was now or never.

The words sounded in his ears, his own when he was
young. He saw himself standing in the barn loft looking out
at the long drop to the pile of hay below. Jump or not jump.
It was now or never.

He was within yards of the cliff when his cell phone rang. He slammed on his brakes. An impulsive reaction to the ringing in his pocket? Or an instinctive desire to go on living?

The pickup slid to a dust-boiling stop, his front tires just inches from the end of the road. Heart in his throat, he looked out at the plunging drop in front of him.

His heart pounded harder. Just a few more moments—a few more inches—and he wouldn't have been able to stop in time.

His phone rang again. A sign? Or just a coincidence? He put the pickup in Reverse a little too hard and hit the gas pedal. The front tires were so close to the edge that for a moment he thought the tires wouldn't have purchase. Fishtailing backward, the truck spun away from the precipice.

Ford shifted into Park and, hands shaking, pulled out his still-ringing phone. As he did, he had a stray thought. How rare it used to be to get cell phone coverage here in the Gallatin Canyon of all places. Only a few years ago the call wouldn't have gone through.

Without checking to see who was calling, he answered it, his hand shaking as he did. He'd come so close to going over the cliff. Until the call had saved him.

"Hello?" He could hear noises in the background. *Hello?* He let out a bitter chuckle. A robocall had saved him at the last moment, he thought, chuckling to himself.

But his laughter died as he heard a bloodcurdling scream coming from his phone.

Get 4 FREE REWARDS!

We'll send you 2 FREE Books <u>plus</u> 2 FREE Mystery Gifts.

Harlequin Intrigue books are action-packed stories that will keep you on the edge of your seat. Solve the crime and deliver justice at all costs.

FREE
Value Over
$20

Love Harlequin romance?

DISCOVER.

Be the first to find out about promotions, news and exclusive content!

f Facebook.com/HarlequinBooks

🐦 Twitter.com/HarlequinBooks

📷 Instagram.com/HarlequinBooks

📌 Pinterest.com/HarlequinBooks

ReaderService.com

EXPLORE.

Sign up for the Harlequin e-newsletter and download a free book from any series at **TryHarlequin.com**

CONNECT.

Join our Harlequin community to share your thoughts and connect with other romance readers! **Facebook.com/groups/HarlequinConnection**